GIRL
TO
GIRL

Illustrated by
George Ulrich

GIRL TO GIRL

The Real Deal on Being a Girl Today

by
Anne Driscoll

ELEMENT
CHILDREN'S BOOKS

SHAFTESBURY, DORSET · BOSTON, MASSACHUSETTS · MELBOURNE, VICTORIA

To the family I helped to begin -
Joe, Maura, Marisa and Colin - as well as
the family that gave me my beginning.

© Element Children's Books 1999
Text © Anne Driscoll 1999
Illustration © George Ulrich 1999

First published in Great Britain in 1999 by
Element Children's Books
Shaftesbury, Dorset SP7 8BP

Published in the USA in 1999 by
Element Books, Inc.
160 North Washington Street,
Boston MA 02114

Published in Australia in 1999 by
Element Books and distributed by
Penguin Australia Limited,
487 Maroondah Highway, Ringwood,
Victoria 3134

Reprinted Febuary, April and October 1999

Cover photograph Dan Smith
Cover design by Ness Wood
Design by The Design Group
Printed and bound in Great Britain by Creative Print and Design
British Library Cataloguing in Publication data available.
Library of Congress Cataloging in Publication data available.

ISBN 1 901881 29 6

ACKNOWLEDGEMENT

Thanks to my editors Barry Cunningham and Michael Powell at Element Children's Books for their steadfast belief in this book and their expertise in shaping it. Thanks to Karen Placzek, also at Element, for her unflagging enthusiasm in getting this book into the hands that would buy it. Thank you to my husband Joe and our children, friends and family for their support, love and guidance. A special acknowledgement to my daughters Maura and Marisa who gave expert advice in the creation of *Girl to Girl*. My gratitude to the teachers, counselors and parents who helped me reach out to girls all over the globe and include their voices. And, finally, a special thanks to the girls themselves. It was their sharing, girl to girl, that made this book happen.

CONTENTS

Chapter 1

Girl to Girl Owning our voices, making our choices **8**

Chapter 2

Friends How to take care of them and keep them **20**

Chapter 3

Boys Friends or enemy? **41**

Chapter 4

Family Where do I belong? **56**

Chapter 5

School What am I learning here? **76**

Chapter 6

Sports and Other Fun Do I throw like a girl? **94**

Chapter 7

My Body and Self-image **109**

What do you see when you look at me? What do I see?

Chapter 8

The Future **124**

Chapter 9

Girl to Girl The real deal on growing up **140**

What's Special About

Girls are great! They're fun, active, interesting, and strong. They're both loud and quiet. They're sweet and silly and serious. Sometimes they are outrageously outgoing and other times they prefer the private space of their own room. Girls are all of these things - and MORE!

As different as girls can be, one thing all girls have in common is concern about their relationships - with their friends, family, teachers, classmates, coaches, and teammates. Fortunately, girls have an amazing amount of insight into their relationships. They watch - sometimes without realizing it - the way their parents are behaving towards each other. They are aware of how a best friend has hurt their feelings, or how they have hurt their best friend. They understand - although may not agree with - their brother's need to show off, or the reasons why

their older sister bosses them around. And as girls are growing up, they are also getting better at handling all those many relationships. Every day - very often without thinking about it - they are practicing all the skills that help them in those relationships, because, their relationships are the most important thing in the world to girls. The biggest challenge for girls is trying to have healthy, strong relationships with the people around them and to balance the needs of those relationships with their own needs.

I believe that girls are really the EXPERTS on their own lives. Girls know what is important to them. They are the ones who feel the frustrations, the fears, the joys, the hopes, the challenges and disappointments that come up in their lives. They understand what makes them happy and what makes them miserable. They know how it feels to be dumped by an old friend, and how great it is to make a new one.

So, this book is really an advice book based on the experience of hundreds of girls who have been willing to share with me what is happening in their lives and in the relationships that are important to them. The girls you will meet in the pages of this book are real girls living real lives in real places. Some are from the United States and some are from the United Kingdom, Australia, and Canada. But no matter where they are from, mostly, they have the same concerns and cares.

Each chapter of this book is organized around a major area of girls' lives, such as family, friends, boys, school, sports. In each chapter, you will meet one girl who shares her experience on that subject, as well as hear the voices of many other girls, too. The book is intended to be fun and interesting and helpful. I hope that in hearing the voices of so many girls, girls will get the impression that, whatever they are experiencing in their own lives, they are not alone.

I hope reading this book will leave you feeling as if you just had a great talk with a friend. And I hope you will be as inspired by the girls who share their lives in this book as I have been.

Anne Driscoll

1 GIRL TO GIRL

Happy

" I'm most happy when I'm with my family or friends. I'm happy then because I'm with someone I know and I can trust. I just like talking most of the time when I'm with them. I get sad when someone close to me turns against me or hurts my feelings. I also feel sad when someone does that to one of my friends or someone in my family. CAITLIN, 11

The times I feel most happy are when I draw - I like to draw. When I have no homework - I feel free. When I play outside or with my family - it's love. When I'm having fun. JENNIFER, 12

The times I feel most happy are when I am with my dad and we go swimming. When I am with my friends and we play heaps of games. When I am sitting down with my mother and my brother and talking, and I also like playing with my brother, you know, throwing balls and stuff, playing board games sort of like Dungeons and Dragons where you make up a character. CAITLIN, 10

I feel happy when I achieve well in Tae Kwon Do, soccer, and schoolwork or when we go camping as a family. REBECCA, 11

I feel most happy on my birthday. And if I was feeling a good feeling. CARMEN, 8 "

Girls rule!

Imagine all the great things there are in your life to do and see and feel and talk about.

Girls' lives have never been better. Today girls have so many choices. From exploring the Internet to rollerblading, there are so many different and exciting ways to spend your time, learn and grow.

Most girls feel great about their lives - most of the time. They like their schools, they enjoy their friends, they love their after-school activities, and really look forward to the time they spend with their families.

Just think. If you were living at the time of your grandmother or great-grandmother, your life would be SO different.

If you lived 80 years ago:

◆ You might not go to school at all because you would have to work to h⏷ your family.

◆ You might be swatted with a paddle or ruler f⏷ disobeying the teacher.

◆ You probably would not go on to college - few women did.

◆ You would have little choice about what job y⏷ might dream of doing. Teaching, nursing, household work, or being a secretary would be about your only choices.

◆ You would have no CDs, TVs, VCRs, or PCs. In fact, you would be very lucky if you⏷ had an electric refrigerator!

really lucky

So girls are really lucky today. They have so much more than any girl living in any other time period has ever had. But that doesn't mean their lives always feel so great. Sometimes you probably feel that your life is the best and other times you might feel like hiding in your closet for the rest of your life!

It's normal to have days where things aren't going well. Days when everything seems to be piling up in a big heap of troubles. Your best friend won't talk to you. You're not even sure she IS your best friend. And you aren't sure how to find out if she is.

Maybe you think you're the only one who feels yucky about her life every once in a while. You might be surprised to know that every girl sometimes feels bad, or sad, or confused. It's TOTALLY normal.

Girls Grow

It does seem, though, that some girls go through life without ever feeling like a geek. They just seem to never have any problems. Their clothes are always so cool. They are always smiling and happy. They always get called on by the teacher. They never have a bad hair day. Their lives seem totally perfect.

Ugggh! It's hard not to be jealous of a girl like that!

I've never had any problems in school because I am a straight-A student. My friends haven't had any problems in school either. KATE, 12

I like school and have fun there because of nice teachers, fun classes, and cool friends. I'm in honors reading, language, arts, and math. STEPHANIE, 12

I have a best friend called Aimee. We've been friends for eight years now. Aimee is great even though we don't go to the same school. She's never let me down. We share secrets and have slumber parties. She's really

cool...

she's really cool...

I probably feel the saddest when somebody belittles me. Last year people teased me a lot and then this year things were going great and I thought they'd grown up when someone said something that made me feel about three inches tall. HEATHER, 12

Whenever my friends are mean, I try not to start fighting. I try to tell them how I feel about it. MAEVE, 10

and has a great attitude. We haven't split up or had a fight for ages and agree on everything. I have other best friends. They're all really nice, as well. I get on well with my other friends. We don't really fight. REBECCA, 11

Some girls do feel happy most of the time. When they think about their lives, they feel good. They feel content to be where they are, glad to be who they are, and happy to be doing what they are. But even girls who are pleased with their lives have times when a problem surfaces that sticks around like an apple peel in your braces. Remember, nobody is happy all the time.

Why?

Well, for one reason, girls change a lot between the time they are eight and when they reach 12 or so. And change can be a challenge! Think about it: at eight, you are probably in first or second or third grade. At that point school is still such a new experience. You are getting better at reading, learning your math facts, and most likely getting to know your way around the school pretty well.

At this age, though, it's still difficult to figure out things like how hard to try to please your teacher and whether being a teacher's pet is good or bad. Some girls worry about their friends, especially if they have friends that are boys. At this age, sometimes other children tease girls about their "boyfriends" instead of understanding they're just "boy friends." At this age, too, some girls may be beginning to see that they are sometimes treated differently just because they ARE GIRLS. This can be really confusing.

Girls continue to grow and change a lot over the next few years. They may notice that a few girls start gathering in their own groups of two or three, maybe calling it a "club", secret or private. Whatever they call it, the purpose of the group seems to be the same: to keep some kids in and others out. If you have ever been an outsider, you know how weird it can feel.

Some girls at school started the JTT club. They'd talk about boys. It was so weird - you had to buy a Bop magazine and it had boy movie stars and stuff. You had to do that to be in the club and I thought it was really stupid - just the whole idea - and not letting anybody in was dumb too. All you do is just stand there. It was really boring actually. So we just didn't join and then it was kind of a blow-out. It just wasn't meeting anymore. It was so weird, it just kind of stopped. MARISA, 11

I am part of a group of four to six people. Basically we hang out at recess (break) so we don't feel like loser loners. HEATHER, 12

Girls Change

That's not all that's happening, either. Some girls feel a lot of pressure, especially from their parents or their teachers. Girls get the message, from their parents and teachers, but also from books, magazines, movies, and television, that they're supposed to be nice, good, sweet. Plus, they're supposed to be pretty. While there isn't anything wrong with being a nice, good, sweet, pretty girl, nobody's perfect. Right?

Then, by the time a girl reaches 12, chances are her body has begun to change. Her body grows taller, her shape changes. Body parts are becoming different. It can feel totally weird and strange. On top of that, there's boys to contend with. Maybe a girl is interested in boys, or maybe she's not. But she's definitely beginning to feel differently about her body, and probably about her relationships with boys.

I have never had a boyfriend before (only in nursery) but I would like one! Sort of. I can talk to boys and I think they can talk to me. I am quite embarrassed talking to boys I fancy. One of my friends had a boyfriend. They sent presents to each other and things like that. CLAIRE, 11

I feel really sad when I'm trying really hard to impress someone, and yet they don't acknowledge my existence. For example, sometimes there is a boy I like and he doesn't even notice me. It makes me feel pretty bad. JESSIE, 12

Another thing that happens as you get older is that you notice that being popular seems to be very important. You could probably pick out the most popular girls (and boys) in a snap, faster than you could say "popularity." How someone gets to be popular, or not, is all part of the social network, that weird system of who's considered the prettiest, most handsome, and coolest.

It's a reality, for sure. And it will affect you to some degree. Maybe you feel good because you have a lot of friends and you feel popular. Maybe you know who the popular kids are but choose to spend your time with other kids - your own friends. Or perhaps the fact that you're not popular really bothers you - a lot.

A time I remember feeling really happy was when a really popular girl in my class mentioned how I have a great sense of humor and how funny I was. It made me feel good deep down because I think I have a wonderful sense of humor and it was time people other than my family realize it!
HEATHER, 12

I have tons of friends, but I'm not really considered to be popular ... none of us are. We just all have a bunch of friends. I guess we're all popular. JESSIE, 12

She's So Popular

Whew! So many things to go through, learn about, and understand. No wonder you might feel confused or upset on occasion. The pressure to be beautiful, act cool, and draw friends to you like a magnet is tough to handle when you feel ugly, dorky, and alone. Times like those can damage your sense of yourself. They can make you doubt who you are and feel awful about what you look like.

The pressure girls feel to be popular sometimes makes them do or say things they are not so proud about. They might talk about someone behind her back to make themselves look better. They might say something mean to the person or snub them in some other way, just to boost their own standing in the group.

My Family?

Girls especially feel concern and worry about their friendships. At times, their friends seem like the most important thing in the world to them. But other relationships are important too. Girls get stressed about their relationships with their teachers, coaches, and most especially, their families.

At age eight, most girls have no doubt their parents are the most important people in the world to them, but by age 12, or so, some

I have been hurt when there are a lot of people and my friends do not play with me. SHIRLEY, 12

There was a new girl and my friend made me feel not wanted. Well, we talked it over so we decided we will all be friends. TIFFANY, 8

There is this girl and hardly anyone likes her so these girls wrote really mean and rude things about her. She started crying and the teachers found out but no one would own up so they had to find out who it was. They compared everyone's handwriting and my handwriting was like the person who had done it, so I got the blame. But then the person owned up. BROOKE, 11

One friend gets mad when I don't want to be in her group. JENNY, 10

I feel sad when people I know are whispering secrets and not telling me. I am also sad when my friends leave me out of different things. ASHLEY, 11

Sara was making fun of one of my friend's weight and I was stuck in the middle. I dealt with it by not going on anyone's side. MAGGIE, 11

girls are now thinking their friends matter more. This may cause tension in a family. But it is by no means the only problem girls have with their parents, step-parents, or brothers and sisters.

What about a pain-in-the-neck little brother? A bossy older sister? A mother who always seems to blame you for everything? A father who doesn't live with you anymore? There are all kinds of things that concern girls about their families.

I get in fights with my brother all the time. Then I apologize and play with him or something. Sometimes my sister and brother get in fights. I sit them down on separate couches and ask them questions to get them to solve it. MARISA, 11

I feel sad when I get in fights with my mom. I feel sad because I love my mom.
SARAH, 12

My big brother always thinks he's right but he's not and he harasses us and harasses us until we give in. I have found out a way to stop him. I put my fingers in my ears and go outside. ALICE, 10

It is not surprising that girls are especially concerned about their relationships with their friends and families and teachers. Experts who study human nature, especially those who have studied girls, find that girls are different from boys, in more ways than just their physical features. The most important thing in the world to girls is their relationships to others: friends, families, teachers, coaches, and others. They want to have strong connections to the people in their lives. Boys, on the other hand, want to show how strong and separate they are from others. They like to be in control and are more aggressive.

One expert studied the way boys and girls played games. If the boys disagreed about some aspect of the game, they considered the rules and continued playing, using the rules as a guide, even if someone was to lose as a result. If girls disagreed about some aspect of the game, they ignored the rules and stopped the game. They didn't want anybody to get hurt and would rather find something else to do than hurt anyone's feelings. This means that girls make different choices and value different things from boys.

Girls Rule

Girls are neat. They can think for themselves, speak up for themselves, solve problems for themselves.

Girls talk. They talk about everything and learn a lot about themselves and their world doing so.

Girls rule. They are interested in the people around them and their relationships with these people. They care about others and are sensitive to their feelings.

My friends are all very different, but in their own way very special to me. I like them all the same most of the time. They're very understanding of other people's likes and dislikes. With some of them I play dolls and we have a great time. We all stick together. STEPHANIE, 12

I got in a fight with my friend about what and where to play. I wanted to go in and she wanted to stay out and play basketball. So I said, "Fine, I'll just go in and play by myself." Then I realized how selfish I was being so I went out and apologized and things worked out. MARISA, 11

I do have a best friend. We have been best friends since we were three years old. We do everything together, we have the same interests. We

It's true... It's true..

don't fight or argue because we always decide together what w[e]
going to do. We are never jealous of each other. REBECCA, 11

It's true. Girls have interesting, exciting lives - more than they've ever been before. You have more opportunities today and in your future than girls your age have ever had. But when there are so many choices, so much pressure, so many interesting people, so much to do and say and talk about, there's bound to be confusion, concerns and cares.

Sarah is a 10-year-old fifth-grade student who is, in many ways, typical of girls her age. Sometimes life is good, sometimes not so great. But mostly, she feels hopeful about her life and her future.

As 10-year-old Sarah says, she feels happy when "someone says something good about me" and sad "when someone dumps on me." She feels school is "sometimes fun but hard." And she feels her family is "nice, loving, caring" but she sometimes has her fights with her brothers that get "settled by our parents." Her friends can "be mean to you sometimes, but nice in other ways, too." About her body, she feels, "I am not overweight and I like myself just the way I am." About her future, she says, "I think about my future when I am in bed. I feel that I will have a good one."

In this book you will find different ways to think about yourself, your life and your future. The girls who share themselves in *Girl to Girl* can help you as you prepare and change and grow.

It's true... It's true...

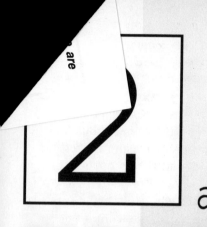

are

How to Take Care of Them and Keep Them

FRIENDS

My best friend is my best friend because we are a very humorous couple and we both tell each other jokes. She's always there for me and I'm always there for her. STEPHANIE, 12

I have a best friend. She is 13, average height and pretty. She is alright at school and sports. She works at the local pet porpoise pool for free. I like her because she is kind, thoughtful and trusting. She respects you for what you are, not for what she wants you to be. ANELIESE, 13

My best friend has two brothers and one sister. She's also in the third grade. She's 10 years old. She's also Spanish. She's my best friend because she's fun to play with and she tells funny jokes. Some of my other friends are mean because if I'm not playing with them they call names. One other friend, she doesn't call me names and she plays with me. She used to go to my school. She's also in the third grade. KEIANA, 8

SARAH Age: 12

I feel most happy when I'm with my friends. It makes me happy because I have lots of fun and feel comfortable. SARAH, 12

I am saddest when I get in fights with my friends. It is hard to get to be friends again. I don't have a specific time but I hate to get in fights with people. Jaclyn is my best friend. She is nice and we always hang out together. Also we share a lot of the same interests. She also helps me out with things and when I'm sad, she makes me feel better. I have other friends too. I like everyone else the same. They are usually all very nice. We sometimes get in fights about dumb things. BRYANNA, 11

Lives with: her mother, a prison administrator, her father, a fireman; her 14-year-old brother, and two sisters, ages seven and eight.

Hobbies: riding her bike, running, kickboxing, swimming, going to the park, and football (soccer).

Favorite hunk: Leonardo DiCaprio – "He's lovely."

Best vacations: DisneyWorld, Universal Studios, and Brittany on the coast of France.

Favorite author: Roald Dahl. "I love The Twits, George's Marvelous Medicine, the BFG."

Favorite music group: Back Street Boys.

Best achievement: being the fastest runner at her old school.

Who do you want to

Who do you want to share your troubles with? Who do you want to spend your spare time, weekends and vacations with? Who do you want to tell your secrets to? A friend, of course. And a best friend is best of all. At least that's life according to 12-year-old Sarah.

Sarah's friends have been with her through good times and bad. They have been there to wipe a tear and comfort her during the roughest waters of her life and have also enjoyed gliding along in her boat in fair weather.

Don't misunderstand. Sarah's family is very important to her. She loves them very much and considers each of them special in their own unique way. She shares a room with her two younger sisters, who fill up one half of the bedroom with their bunk beds, Barbies, and flutes, while Sarah has the other half of the bedroom, lined with Leonardo DiCaprio posters all over the walls. Her brother is okay too, although she says he is totally mad about music. And her parents? "My mum is caring, loving and a great mum. My dad is funny, embarrassing me in front of my friends, but a big softie."

Yet in spite of the closeness and love she feels for her family, they can never be what her friends are for her. That is very different. Life is just a lot better if you get to spend it with friends. For sure, our families are the first set of people we relate to. But after our families, the most important relationships we have are with our friends.

Where do we meet the strangers who become friends? **everywhere!**

When we were younger, we might have met them at the sandbox or playgroup or daycare center. As we get older, we find friends in our neighborhood, at our school, on our sports teams, at music lessons, in our after-school program, or at summer camp. Let's face it - **girls are everywhere**. So the possibilities for finding friends is infinite - as in, endless.

A best friend

tell your secrets to?

I do like everyone and I don't really have a best friend because we have to learn when we are growing up what being a friend really means.
VICTORIA, 8

I don't have a best friend as I think it's slightly silly because if your friend moves or you have a massive fight, you have no one else to be with. I personally have lots of "best friends." Most of my best friends are girls and they all have great personalities and all are different (which is good). I have two really close friends which are boys and they are both really nice. JOLENE, 12

I have more than one best friend but these people are all different and I like them all for different reasons. I can tell each of them different things and we get along very well. People who are just my friends I may not trust as much as my best friends. I may not hang around with them as much as my best friends. ALI, 13

When I feel sad is when my friends are not here at the time. JESSICA, 9

Sarah has quite a few friends she counts on, as well as a couple of true blue "best friends." At school, there is a whole group of people with whom she is friends. "We're quite friendly in our class," she explains. This group is very sociable with each other. They talk and joke together. They share their lunches and sometimes their secrets. Her friends at school are all different and she enjoys them for their differences. But the one thing all her friends share with Sarah is talking together. Talking is what girls do!

"Friends are really important - you need someone to talk to. You need to hang around with people as well," says Sarah.

But how do you know who is a friend and who isn't?

"You have to be able to trust them. They can't just go off and pick

is best of all

on you sometimes. You have to be kind of friendly because otherwise you feel uncomfortable or stuff. You need to know you can talk to them about your problems," says Sarah.

In other words, the biggest thing between friends next to **talking** is **trusting!** They go hand in hand. You share, they share. You share a little more, they share a little more. Little by little, you're learning to trust each other. That's called relating! And that's what friendship is really all about. Amazing, isn't it?

Besides her chums at school, Sarah also has other friends that she sees after school, especially the ones who go to the club at the park near her house. Some of them live in her neighborhood and Sarah might kick the soccer ball a bit with them. Or Sarah hops on her bike and pedals down to the park where the club house is. There, there are organized activities such as the time they made banners to hang on the club house or spruced up the building with a new paint job.

- Don't ask too many personal questions at first.
- Be friendly.
- Talk to them in an interested, nice way.

Best Friends, Best Buds

Siobhan is one of Sarah's "best friends." "I've known her all my life. My mum and dad have been best friends with her parents and we got to be best friends as well. We do fight with each other sometimes but we say we're really sorry," explains Sarah.

Siobhan is two years older than Sarah, but it doesn't really matter. They share a lot in common and feel soooooo close to each other. They accept one another. And they really care about each other. Because their parents are friends, they sometimes get to travel together, which makes their friendship extra special, like the time Sarah and Siobhan went with their families to Florida together, trekking through Universal Studios, Busch Gardens, and DisneyWorld.

The great thing about their friendship is that Sarah and Siobhan each realize that they have other "best friends" too. They don't really get jealous. They understand they have different sets of friends when they're apart and they make room for them. "I've had a few arguments with her but we've patched them up," says Sarah.

My best friend is pretty, cool, and smart.
ROBIN, 9

What makes Siobhan so special? She's funny, she's trustworthy, and she knows how to keep a secret. Plus, how many people can you claim to have known **your whole life?**

"

Denira is the best because she helps me feel strong but Karsia is one of my best friends because she is funny. TIFFANY, 8

I do have a best friend. She is my best mate because she is always there for me. All I've got to do is phone her and she will come out and talk to me and see what's the matter. I'm always there for her as well. DONNA, 12

I do have a best friend. We get into fights and at this very moment she won't talk to me. Her name is Katie. She is my best friend because we share many interests. We have a lot of the same characteristics of the way we act. Overall she is very nice and trustworthy and I can tell her everything.

Although we are in a fight right now, regardless, she is my best friend. She says I am mean to her, that she hates me and she doesn't want to be my best friend anymore. The way I am dealing with this is I'm trying to give her space and talk to her to try to work it out.

I think that you should only have one best friend. However, I have another closest friend aside from Katie. We were best friends in fifth grade but gradually we drifted apart because we made new friends and those new friends became our best friends. At this point, we spend a lot of time fighting, mostly because of silly things, for example, lip gloss, pens, attitudes, etc. Sometimes I wonder if this is just a big stage we're going through as part of growing up and being mature. GINA, 12

I do have a best friend. She is my best friend because she listens to me, she keeps secrets and I can trust her. I can talk to her about anything. I have lots of other friends. All of my friends are kind. I don't really have another best friend because I like everybody. CLAIRE, 12

"

Best Friend

For Sarah, her other best friend is Vicky, who is the same age as Sarah and from the same town, but is now going to a different school. Hard to believe, but when Sarah first met Vicky, they were enemies. They didn't really like each other at all, but eventually, they started getting to know each other better, and duh! Now they're best friends.

"My best friend is Vicky because she is trusting, funny, easy to get on with, and she trusts me. When I was younger - when I was six - we were enemies and used to go home crying some days, but now we are best friends and I hope it stays that way," says Sarah.

Sarah and Vicky live about five streets apart, so they might go to the cinema, swimming, shopping, or play down the park together. Sometimes they go to a theme park that's not too far away from where they live. But has being at separate schools all day been a problem? "No way!" says Sarah.

"I used to go to the same school as Vicky but I couldn't get into the school she went into. I wanted to go there since some of my other friends are there as well, but I live a bit farther from that school so I couldn't get in," says Sarah. "Being at different schools has made us a bit closer, I think. We phone each other up and we have a lot of things to talk about."

So Sarah and Vicky share what's happening at their different schools, how they like their teachers, their classes and what's going on with their different sets of friends. Sarah says it's not always easy to be best friends with someone who has other friends as well.

"Sometimes she goes out and she doesn't ask me and sometimes I do the same. We're about the same when it comes to jealousy. Sometimes she feels left out and sometimes I do. You wonder, what are they doing now. That's what you're thinkng about," says Sarah.

But, there's enough trust to eventually work things out. And talking about things is what really makes that happen, Sarah says.

What makes a best

Rate these qualities 1 to 10 (1 being the most important and 10 the least):

_____ she tells you what you want to hear
_____ she's pretty
_____ she's honest
_____ she can keep a secret
_____ she has a strong sense of humor
_____ she's a good listener
_____ she's someone you admire
_____ she lives near you
_____ you have a lot of interests in common
_____ she tells you her secrets

I have two best friends. They are my best friends because they have a good sense of humor and are nice to me. I feel like they would never ditch me for anything else. We almost never get in fights. Besides my two best friends, I don't really have any other best friends. I just have good friends. That is because most of the time they are really nice to me but they aren't as trustworthy. I had a problem with one of my best friends but because she is my best friend it only lasted one day. It hurt my feelings because we were both trying to get people on our sides and that was rude, but we were both very upset with each other. We solved it by talking it through on the phone. LINDSAY, 12

I do have a best friend. I consider her my best friend for many reasons. She is always there for me, to support me and stuff. She knows how to have fun and create a good time out of something. I admire the way that she is so confident about things and so kind toward everyone. I have other good friends but not any best friends. I don't close myself up to be with only one person. I am friends with a ton of other people. I feel that if you want a strong relationship with a friend, fighting helps to build strength between you. Anyway, once last

year, our school team went away to an overnight at a camp. My best friend and I had spent a ton of time together and I guess we just got sick of each other. We got in an argument over the color of a toothbrush. We solved it by having other people mediate us. EMILY, 11

My best friend is Kelly because she is nice when I need someone to tell something to. JENNY, 10

Friends Can Help

Probably one of the worst things that's ever happened to Sarah is when her dog died. She didn't think she could ever get through the experience. And if it hadn't been for the comfort and caring of her friends, she might not have. There had been other family pets that had died before Jasper. Two rabbits that died quite a long time ago. Several guinea pigs, too. A hamster named Sammy that lived to age three when most die at two and a half. But Jasper, Sarah's nine-year-old yellow Labrador, was special. He was like another member of the family to Sarah.

Sarah loved to snuggle with Jasper. He was so faithful, such a good friend to her. He was always there for her when she'd come home from school, or when she'd return from playing with her friends. But then Jasper got sick. The vet told Sarah that he had cancer. The little pup she had played with and palled around with from the time he was six weeks old was very sick and would not get better.

"He's like a brother to me, really. I was quite upset. I've been crying a lot, as well. I know he'll be happier now because he was in a lot of pain. It's better for him to be put down. Now he'll be happier because he's in heaven. I didn't really want to see him be put down, though," Sarah recalls.

The pain of it all was just awful. She couldn't concentrate on anything but the thought of Jasper. His sweet face would appear in her mind and she'd feel sunken by the weight of all her grief. Sarah was so upset she couldn't go to school. She was afraid she would break down, drowning in a puddle of tears - right in front of everyone!

Friends Help ...
... make you feel better
... you study for a tough test
... you get over a hurt
... by listening to your darkest secrets
... you fix your worst bad hair day ever!
... you become yourself!

Who came to her rescue? Vicky was first to the scene. The night after Jasper died, Sarah went to Vicky's house to tell her the bad news. "She was quite upset. She liked him and she's known him all the time that we've been friends. She's quite upset and that's quite nice to know that she's upset as well. I'm not pleased she's upset, but it's good to know she cares and she's got feelings for my family too - for my sisters, my brother, she really likes my mum and dad. It's quite nice."

Everyone has disappointments in life. The A they didn't get on a test. The team they didn't make. The squabble they had with a parent. Sometimes everyone feels hurt, pain, sadness, and grief. What helps us get through those times is the caring and concern of a good friend.

What Best Friends Say About Each Other

Alex and Maeve:

I am most happy when I play with my friend because she is funny and caring. I felt the saddest when my fish died (his name was Aqua) because I loved him very much and I missed him. Actually all my friends are my best friends but I have a really good friend. She is always happy and nice. My relationships with my other friends are good, fun, and funny. All of my friends are funny and exciting at times, but in all, they are the neatest friends anybody could have. Sometimes I get in fights with some of my friends and I just ignore them but in about five minutes we are friends again. ALEX, 10

I feel the happiest when I am with all my friends. I felt very sad when my pet dog Sandy died. There was nothing to do around the house after she was gone. One of my best friends is Alex. She is one of my best friends because she is nice and not selfish. I have about 3 million best friends. They are all nice, kind, caring, and generous. Whenever I seem to need them, they are always there. MAEVE, 10

Anna and Karen:

I feel most happy when I am hanging out with my friends, at an amusement park, or around my cat Miko. I feel the saddest when I get in big arguments with my friends. Don't worry, we always make up. I have a best friend. Her name is Karen. We both love animals, have cats, are outgoing and just like to have fun. We also have a plan to keep in touch and when we get older be roomies and have lots of pets. We're also saving up now for a car, for when we're teens. We have a lot of fun together. I have other best friends and they are nice. Some are crazy and some are shy. I am crazy. My "very best friend" Karen is nicer than other people. Best friends are good friends, but then there's "very best friends" which are different.
ANNA, 10

I feel happiest when I'm with animals or my cat Brian and my best friend. I like doing fun stuff with my friends. I have a best friend. Her name is Anna. We both are alike and love animals. And we like doing crazy stuff and having fun and doing makeup and face masks. When me and Anna grow up we will, if we can, keep in touch. We will buy a house and fill it with animals from the Humane Society and other different kinds of animals we like. And we will breed endangered animals. I have other best friends. They are nice and sometimes crazy. But my favorite friend is Anna because she's more like me and we never got in a fight. KAREN, 10

Friends Can Hurt

If you're lucky and you have good friends that are dependable and trustworthy, they will be there when you need them. But friendships are like living, breathing things. They can change over time. Sometimes they can bite.

"When I was younger a girl called Tess used to live down my road and we used to go round each other's house all the time. Then one day, her friend from school came round when I was there and she didn't like me so she punched me and I started crying because she was three years older than me and quite big. Tess just stood there laughing so I went home and told my mum and dad and they went and talked to her mum. She said she wouldn't do a thing like that and now that I have moved, I haven't seen her in ages," says Sarah.

That was a tough lesson for Sarah: sometimes the person you think you know isn't always who they seem. It can be totally weird when that happens. It can make you feel like: duh! How come I didn't see that coming?

unintended

But anyone can have a bad day, or make a mistake, or say something they regret later, or hurt someone they really care about. Sometimes it's just a case of thoughtlessness. Sometimes it's unintended. Sometimes it's spite. But whatever the hurt that happens between friends, it can mean pain.

"Some girls whisper about each other. What are they whispering about? They start laughing and look at you. I just don't worry about it. I don't really mind if they talk about me. I'm not going to have a go at them for it. Sometimes I do get my friends to ask what they're talking about but they don't say anything. I just leave it. No point in worrying about it. It's just what girls do. Gossiping is normal. They need something to talk about," Sarah explains.

What do you do if a friend hurts you?

Q. I have a best friend, but I sometimes think she's talking about me. What should I do?

A. The fact that you feel uncomfortable means there's a problem with trust. The best thing to do may be to talk to her and if she doesn't seem to care, then she is probably not a friend at all.

Q. My friend sometimes ignores me, especially if there's a certain other girl around that she really likes. It makes me feel awful. And mad, too! Should I tell her how I feel?

A. A friend should always be careful to protect their friends' feelings, try to be sensitive to their needs and not hurt them. Perhaps she doesn't realize that she's ignoring you or that she's making you feel bad. Try and talk it over with her.

Q. My best friend likes to gossip about other people. It makes me feel like she could be gossiping about me too. Am I crazy, or what?

A. No, you are perfectly sane. And smart, too. Tread carefully, she could be untrustworthy to you too!

Q. I just had a huge fight with my best friend over something totally stupid. What do I do now?

A. Give yourself and your friend some space. Spend some time apart, think it over; sooner or later you'll end up talking again. Most likely you'll get over it and get back together.

The best advice you'll ever need about friends: show your friends they need you more than you need them!

Emily is my best friend because I have known her since I was a month old. We have fallen out many times over things from her ignoring me to great rows over us being totally horrid to each other. CHARLOTTE, 12

I have been hurt lots of times by friends, but we would work it out. One time my friend Emily would always talk about her best friend. One day I told her to please stop talking about her. Most of the time she can't control her anger. So she insulted me. So I left. After a few days of not talking to each other, she said, 'Sorry.' And we both sat down to work it out. MAYA, 11

I was hurt by a friend but not by words. If it was by words I wouldn't have cared. It was by hand. She hit me because I was talking to someone she didn't like. I ignored her and said, "I can play with anyone I please. You're not a real friend if you don't approve of who I am friends with. You can still be my friend but you don't control me." SUKI, 11

I haven't physically been hurt by a friend but I've had my feelings hurt. One of my friends at my last school was a user. She just picked and person and they'd be her friend for a day. I used to be bullied but she just got bored and stopped. REBECCA, 11

What About Me?

Have you ever felt left out? It is that same feeling as when you get picked last for the team at school recess. It is an awful feeling, but girls are strong and others have made it through the same thing okay. It's no fun being ignored, overlooked, passed by. In fact, it feels absolutely dreadful.

You can feel like an outsider for many reasons. Because you didn't get invited to join a group of girls going to the mall. Because there's no room for you at the lunch table. Because no one told you it was crazy hat day at school!

For Sarah, one of the times when she felt out of place was when she switched to her new school. It was one of the hardest transitions she had ever faced because most of her friends were going to a different school together and she didn't know many people. But she did what any quick-witted, cordial, resourceful girl would do: She made new friends.

My friend is very weird. For instance she was playing with me on Saturday and on Sunday she went off with her other friend and ignored me so I thought she didn't like me. So I called her and said, "What are you playing at?" I said, "I know you are allowed other friends but you shouldn't have left me out." DONNA, 12

How did she do it?

"Sometimes I sit next to people and we just start talking about things and gradually we started becoming friends. We sit at tables of four ... I just made friends quite quickly," says Sarah.

Stuck in Between

It happens to everyone. We've all been in the middle of a fight. The best thing to do is to step back and let them solve the problem, since it's not your issue, it's theirs. If you think you can help mediate it, help, but don't get caught on one side or the other. That's a bad move that will definitely put you in a bad place.

I feel saddest when my friends don't call me or don't invite me places or when I get a bad grade. Once when everyone went to my friend's house, she didn't invite me because her mom said she couldn't have anyone else over. I was really upset. DANYA, 14

I feel most happy going to the mall and hanging out with friends and being around my friends. I feel the saddest when all my friends and family are so busy and I'm just here at home. MAGGIE, 11

I do have a best friend. She has long brown hair and is very enthusiastic. She is my best friend because I can always talk to her, no matter what. My relationships with my other best friends are very good. They are very nice and hopeful. I have had problems with a friend. A bunch of girls and I lied to one friend and we got into a big fight and at the end we all became friends. Another time some of my friends were in a fight and I was stuck in the middle. I solved it by not taking sides and not talking to them. JACQUELYN, 12

Popular Pals

◆ It's never ever a good idea to step over your friends to get in with people you see as popular.

◆ It doesn't matter whether you and your friends are popular. It matters whether you enjoy each other's company, treat each other well, and have fun together.

◆ Popular people may not always stay that way. If they are nasty and use their popularity like a whip, chances are their status won't last till high school!

Sarah has learned a lot about being a friend and having friends. She's learned through her relationship with her two best friends that it's great to laugh with someone, great to listen to someone, great to be cared for by someone. But she's also learned that not everyone can be a best friend, because that's a very special friend that has earned the most special trust.

Sarah has lots of other friends too. They're not necessarily her best friends, but they are good friends to pal around with just the same. She enjoys sitting at lunch with them or meeting after school at the park.

Sarah has been hurt by friends and helped by them. But through it all, she's learned to deal with it. Her true friends have been there for her when she's needed them the most. Sarah is not sure she will get another dog. No dog could be like Jasper because Jasper is unique. But she is sure she will continue to make new friends in her life, even as she works to keep the ones she has. For her, making friends is like anything else in life: the more you do it, the better you get at it.

I have two equal best friends. I like them because they don't care if I'm popular or not. They like me for who I am. I really only have one other friend. Most of the other people see me through the eyes of nothing. The reason is I'm not very popular. I think people who are popular aren't nice to people all the time. So it doesn't matter to me if I'm popular or not. A good amount of my friends left me for more popular people. I just think to myself, it doesn't matter, there are many other people. I am still nice to them. SHANNON, 11

Are you a good friend?

1. A friend of yours starts talking about your "best friend", spreading bad rumors about her. You ...

A. Pretend you didn't hear her say anything.

B. You tell her that's not true and stop talking about my friend.

C. You tell other people what you've heard.

2. Your friend calls you, crying on the telephone. She's so upset that you can't even understand what she's saying. You ...

A. Just keep on saying, "Yes. That's too bad. I'm so sorry."

B. Say you'll come right over.

C. Tell her you are expecting another telephone call and you'll call her back.

3. Your friend asks you to hang around, but you have other plans. You ...

A. Tell her you can't but you lie to her about why and she finds out.

B. Tell her you're sorry, you'd love to but you have other plans.

C. Tell her you'd rather hang out with another friend.

4. Your friend tries on a new outfit and asks you how it looks and you know she'd look better dressed in a paper bag. You ...

A. Tell her it looks okay.

B. Say that maybe it isn't the right look for her and suggest another outfit.

C. Tell her she'd look better dressed in a paper bag.

5. Your friend's pants split in gym. She is totally humiliated. You ...

A. Look at her sympathetically and then talk to her later.

B. Go over to her and tell her you'll go with her to her locker so she can change.

C. Laugh along with everyone else.

If your answers were mostly As, then you're a pretty good pal. But try hard and you could be an even better best friend!

If your answers were mostly Bs, you're the best friend a best friend could ask for.

If your answers were mostly Cs, you need to work a little harder at your friendships. Kindness is key, here!

Kindness is the key

3

BOYS

FRIENDS

OR ENEMY

Boys! Well, my relationship with boys is a friendship. I get on with boys as if they are my friend. I have had relationships where it's boyfriend and girlfriend but it doesn't work. So I just stay friends with them.
JOLENE, 12

Boys? Lots of boys are nice to me. I like them a lot. During school I walk with some girls and boys to classes. On our way, we'd fool around and laugh. I wouldn't call them my boyfriend or anything. It makes me feel like they think of me as a friend. And I like that feeling. MAYA, 11

I have had two boyfriends before. One called Michael and one called Thomas. I have known Michael from nursery and we were nearly always in the same class. We had on and off relationships all through junior school. We were friends from the start of school. Thomas asked me out while we were at a swimming pool. I was with my friends and he was with his. I didn't know what to say! In the end, I said yes. I now fancy a boy called Chris. I think he is really nice. DONNA, 12

Well, I don't really like boys but some of them I have second thoughts about. SHIRLEY, 12

I like boys sometimes, but if they are obnoxious and rude, I can't stand them. If they are sweet and caring, I love them to bits. VICTORIA, 12

Why do young boys my age like to hit me instead of communicating nicely? I dislike boys. They are always picking on me and even though I try to be nice to them, most boys annoy me to death. VICTORIA, 8

CHRISTINE Age: 11

Lives with: her mother, a bookkeeper, and father, who's at home with Christine and her 10-year-old sister.

Hobbies: soccer, tap-dancing, clarinet, and chorus.

Favorite author: Lois Lowry.

Favorite book: Number the Stars.

Favorite subject: science. Loves to look at the stars and study astronomy.

Favorite computer game: playing Tetris with a friend. "We do it for fun and try to get a higher score."

Pet peeve: "My sister's stuffed animals. She loves animals and she has more than 100 of them in her bed. They're everywhere and I usually have to pick them up. She has really, really big ones and really, really small ones and they're all over the floor."

At the age of 11, Christine hasn't had a boyfriend,

although she has had boy friends. And there's a really big difference, she says.

Boys can seem like totally weird alien creatures that are difficult to understand and even harder to get to know. Some girls think of boys as the enemy - the kind that chases them at recess, teases them at the bus stop, or cuts ahead of them in the lunch line. But, if girls are lucky, they might even count boys among their friends.

"I do have some friends who are boys. I can talk to them and ask them things and they can do the same with me. I like this because then I can see a different point of view from a different gender. I have always wanted to have a boy friend who I can tell secrets to and I'd be able to trust him. But I don't think I'd want to go out with him," says Christine.

Are boys and girls different? Duh! Of course they are. There are many physical differences between boys and girls, as well as differences at the rate and ways their bodies and minds grow and change. For example, you may have noticed that girls tend to mature faster than boys. The girls you know probably learned to read earlier and mastered math concepts sooner than your boy classmates. Maybe right now there are quite a few girls in your class that tower over the boys. These differences are a result of the natural way our bodies and brains grow.

But there are other, less visible ways that boys and girls differ. These differences are not so much because of the way boys and girls are born, but the way the world treats each sex and what it expects of them.

If you're a girl, you may have noticed that making friends and being friends with a boy is different than being friends with a girl. Have you ever wondered why? Experts who are looking at the ways boys and girls develop and grow up now believe that both girl and boy babies come into the world wanting the same thing: relationships. For example, both boys and girls are born with an intense strong desire to connect with their mothers, and the other people around them. But at about age four or five, boys begin to get sidetracked. They start getting the message from movies, TV, video games, and other influences that to be a strong boy - one that's going to grow to be a stronger man - their relationships are not as important as being independent and aggressive. Have you ever noticed the way some boys show off? Like to be in charge? Won't admit to feeling weak? With boys, it's important to remember that what you see on the outside does not always match with what they're feeling on the inside.

I don't have that many friends that are boys. I chose that decision because you never know when they are going to be nice or not. They are very unpredictable. LINDSAY, 12

One boy likes me. One day my aunt took me to his house and we played outside. He said to me he loved me and he pushed me. JENNY, 10

At my age, we think boys are disgusting! GILLIAN, 8

I don't really think boys like me but I've had a few boyfriends. They're hard to deal with because they're so immature! I try my best. DANYA, 14

I don't see a lot of boys anymore, as I go to an all girls' school. But when I was in primary school all the boys thought they were the best. But I didn't care because they are just boys and boys that think they're the best do stupid things. MARIA, 11

Besides Christine's best friend, who thinks she's really funny, she has a number of other close girlfriends who understand and accept her. This year Christine and four of her friends decided to take a tap/jazz dance class together. It was there that Christine also made friends with two boys who took the class.

"Four other friends of mine - we decided we wanted to do something together. So we took this dance class. Two other boys joined the class. One's in eighth grade and one's in seventh. One of them, he's really into acting and drama. He can really juggle and we recently had a class play and he was the main character. He's really good. I've seen him downtown and I say hi to him. Then the other boy joined the class and it was kind of a relief for the other one," says Christine.

Taking a dance class gives both the boys and girls a shared experience, something in common, although it doesn't always build a total bridge between the boys and girls.

"It's kind of harder to talk to boys. With girls, you know what it's like (to be a girl). With boys, you don't know what it's like so it's harder. I can talk to them, I'm just not as comfortable and I'd rather talk to girls," says Christine.

Christine, like many girls, find boys a total mystery. There are so many things she doesn't understand about them. Why do they enjoy telling each other gross things? What's the deal with wrestling and pushing each other all the time? Why do they love Nintendo so much?

"I wonder what they think about? What they do for fun? Why they all play sports? Why they don't dance? The boys in my dance class are into acting and dance, they aren't the sporty type. So they're different than the other boys," says Christine.

Can You Imagine A Boy...

... Crying on your shoulder because he got a C on his English test?

... Calling you up and asking you why you wouldn't sit with him at lunch?

... Gossiping about what his friend wore to school that day?

... Suggesting that you and he stay in and talk rather than go outside and play?

... Asking to borrow a pair of jeans?

... Styling your hair in a totally awesome new hairstyle? Then painting your nails with little flowers? (Hard to imagine isn't it?!)

Christine thinks that boys probably don't understand very much about girls, either. She says they probably wonder: "Why we have to be nice? Why girls wear makeup? Why they're always talking with each other? Why they're talking so much? Why girls feel like they have to be pretty? Why they don't have self-esteem?"

The researchers who study the way boys and girls grow up think that many of the differences we see between boys and girls reflect the differences in the ways we are brought up, not in our biology. Those very real - although learned - differences, though, make us curious about each other. Most girls really do want to get to know boys better. (And vice versa, too!)

And there's so much to understand about one another! At recess, for example, during a basketball game between boys and girls, Christine has watched how the boys don't really pass to each other - they'd rather make the basket and get the glory for themselves!

"Usually we play boys against the girls. Then we don't have to pick teams and no one will be picked last. That wouldn't be fair. The boys say, 'Let's pick teams.' But the girls say, 'Let's not.' Sometimes on my soccer team we'll scrimmage boys the same age group as the girls, but not in the same division. They always try and show off in front of the girls, trying to do a good move, and they mess up. They try to score goals, kick it as hard as they can, they don't really play well together. They're trying to be the best and show off, so the girls win. Last year we always used to scrimmage with the boys and we never lost to them. We'd usually win or tie ...We have to shake hands afterward and sometimes the boys would try to slap your hand really hard," explains Christine.

The most common place for girls and boys to have contact, of course, is in school. Let's face it, unless you go to an all girls' or all boys' school, most girls and boys are stuck in classrooms together for six hours a day. Often, they have no choice but to get to know each other.

How to get to know a boy

So how's your team doing?

- Start a conversation with him. Ask him about something he enjoys, like, "How's your soccer team doing this season?" Or, "What's the computer club working on these days?"
- Volunteer to work on a class project together.
- Organize an activity like a basketball match, touch-football game, volleyball competition, or ping-pong tournament for a group of your friends and his.
- If he's on a sports team, go to one of his games. Show an interest in what he does.
- Throw a party. Invite him, his friends and yours. It could be a barbecue, a make-your-own-pizza party, or a who-can-make-the-best-ice-cream-sundae contest.

In Christine's class, for example, the students are asked to discuss current events. The talk is usually lively and fun and often wanders off into different subjects. It also gets both the boys and girls talking together. "It's brought us closer together," says Christine. "This year we have assigned seats and girls and boys are together. If you're next to them, you have to talk to them."

Christine has become good friends with a boy she sits next to in homeroom. **She thinks he is nice.**

"Sometimes I talk to him. Sometimes he talks to me about soccer because I play and he says he's going to play. We're pretty close," says Christine. "You can get a different point of view with a boy. It's someone you can laugh with or talk with and you can trust. The kid who sits next to me, I've sat next to all year, I've grown close to him, but I can't tell him really private stuff."

Okay, maybe not really private stuff, but they are so close that when he decided he liked two of Christine's friends, it was Christine he asked to send a message to them both. She finds that that is often the way boys try to get the attention of girls they like. Maybe it's because sending a messenger is not quite as scary as talking to the girl yourself.

Well! I like boys as in friends but not love stuff. We don't go out in our school. We're just all friends. BROOKE, 11

Boys are real idiots. If they want to go out with someone, they have a messenger. If you want to go out with someone, do it yourself. No boy has ever asked me out. I would say no, but like everyone else has been asked out, it seems, and I'm jealous - even though I would not do it. ANDREA, 12

My relationships with boys are okay. I have met two boys. They are brothers and they have both asked me out. And they have asked out my friend as well. I like them. I am a bit shy with boys. KAYLEIGH, 11

My friendship with boys is okay. I am not dating yet but do have boys as some of my friends. Most of my friends say boys are the enemy but some of us feel differently. AMY, 12

I have many boys who are friends. Although I do have a boyfriend named Paul. Paul is very nice, funny and cute. I think that it is alright to have a relationship with boys, as long as you respect each other. Paul and I have a very strong and good relationship and it keeps building. EMILY, 11

So, as if life isn't complicated enough already! Girls are not only busy handling their relationships with other girls, they're also exploring their relationships with boys. Somewhere between ages eight and twelve, chances are many girls are wanting to nudge their friendships with boys along. They might flirt with boys. Write notes to their friends about cute ones in their class. Or (GASP!) talk to boys on the telephone.

What's Up with That?

A "crush" can appear out of nowhere, just like a bolt of lightning. And just like lightning it can send a high-voltage current up your spine - ZAP! You know, you see HIM walking toward you and you think, "Geez! Did I just stick my finger in an electric socket? Otherwise, why on earth do I feel so tingly?"

What to do? Wait and check your temperature later. This buzz you feel may pass. Or, then again, this spark may turn into something bigger.

Whew! How things change! One minute boys are a pox on the face of the earth, and the next, they're your newest interest. This change can happen quickly.

"It's harder to be a girl because of the peer pressure to like boys. Ever since we came into the middle school, people have been asking people to go out with them - like boyfriend/girlfriend. If you don't, people say, 'Come on. I think you should go out with so and so.' It catches on and it's really hard to say no. It's happened to me. I don't really like it, but they say, 'I think you should go out. You two would be a good couple.' But I don't really want to. My really good friends might ask me one time and walk away, but they stop. Sometimes it's other girls pressuring you, but more often it's the boy or the boy's friends," says Christine.

When people "go out," Christine says they might walk downtown together or go to the skating rink, sometimes with a group of other people. Sometimes they just talk on the phone together.

The pressure to "go out" with someone can be tough, especially if more than one of his friends are pushing a girl at the same time. "They say, 'He really really likes you. You'll break his heart if you don't go out with him.' Sometimes I think they're exaggerating just to get you to go out," says Christine.

When it happened to Christine, she just said no. "I just felt I was too young to go out. I didn't like him in a romantic kind of way ... I was really surprised that would happen in fifth grade. I thought that wouldn't happen until eighth grade."

So why do girls and boys go out so often before they're really ready? Sometimes people think it will make them seem cool to their classmates (or themselves) to be doing something so grown-up. It might be a way of getting attention from another boy - and the other kids, too.

Questions

After one boy called the house a number of times and her parents began asking questions, Christine talked to her mom about it. She said that she didn't mind if Christine was friends with boys, but she hoped she would wait until she was older to start going out. She told Christine she wouldn't have anything to look forward to when she got older.

My relationship is quite good with boys. I have a boyfriend. He plays in my brother's football team. We meet through my brother really. He introduced me to him and I just couldn't believe my eyes. He is really cute. He has blue eyes, blond hair, and a cute face. GEORGIA, 12

51

I don't have any relationship with any boys.
A few of my friends do, though. SHANNON, 11

My relationships with boys are good. I have been out with a few boys and my relationships have been great. I fancy a boy now. His name is Jack. I really want to go out with him. I think he is sexy. My first kiss was with a boy called Steven. He's a good kisser. I would love to kiss Jack and feel how soft his lips are. CLAIRE, 12

I'm still too young to be worrying about boys so they're only my friends. TIFFANY, 8

I had a friend. When I broke up with my boyfriend, two minutes later she went out with him. I was mad. JADE, 12

Have you ever had a best friend, then you make a new friend and your best friend gets hurt and jealous? It happens, for sure. And it happens not just between girlfriends but also between girlfriends and boyfriends. People feel possessive over the people they care about. Your girl friends might be hurt that if you're paying more attention to the boys, you might be paying less attention to the girls. The challenge for girls is to try to balance what your needs are (to try a different kind of relationship, for example) with your other needs (to maintain your relationship with your best friend).

Let's admit it. Growing up and managing all these developing relationships (with boys and girls) is a lot like rollerblading for the first time. You have to figure out how the wrist guards go on, adjust your helmet to your particular head, and buckle up your rollerblades. The first time you stand up in them, it's more than a little bit scary. You feel nervous and unsure of yourself. You probably will fall - **more than once!** That's okay. If you haven't failed, you'll never succeed because you're not trying hard enough. It's the same way with your relationships with boys, and girls, for that matter. There's a lot of ground to cover, and you're wearing roller blades. Eventually, you're going to get better at cruising along with confidence.

And as with anything else you're trying for the first time, it's often better not to try it alone. That's why it's not uncommon for boys and girls to enjoy each other's company in groups. It's easier that way, since it's more comfortable and less talk.

Christine says that some of her friends have tried "going out" with boys, and have decided they didn't really like it. Maybe they just feel they're not ready for it. Maybe they haven't found a boy they really feel comfortable with. Or perhaps they're just waiting to be a little bit older, a little bit bolder.

What should you do if a boy likes you?

1. First of all, decide what you think of him. Do you like him? In what way? As an acquaintance? Good friend? Possible boyfriend?

2. Ask yourself what kind of relationship you feel most comfortable with. Weigh whether or not you enjoy his company: (A) with other friends; (B) alone.

3. Decide whether or not you feel you can trust this boy. How well do you know him? Many girls feel the best kind of relationship with a boy is one that starts out as a friendship first, and then grows from there.

4. If you think that he is someone you'd like to get to know better, then enjoy his company.

Awesome

DATING
DATING
Q's DATING A's
DATING

Q. What's the right age to date?

A. The right age to date is when you and your parents feel comfortable with that decision.

Q. What exactly is a "date"? Is it kissing, or what?

A. A "date" is when two people spend time together to get to know each other better. Kissing is not necessary, nor always advisable, either!

Q. Should I ask a boy out if I like him? What if he says no?

A. Sure, ask away - if you really are ready. While it's true he could say no, it would be his loss if he did. In that case, find someone else who appreciates you!

Q. I think I'm ready to date, but my parents don't. What should I do?

A. It wouldn't be wise to go against their wishes. By asking them for permission to date, you're asking them to trust you. Being deceitful will only make it harder for them to trust you again.

Q. Is it better to get to know a boy one-on-one, or as part of a group of friends, going someplace and doing something together?

A. While it's nice to be able to talk privately with a boy, many girls feel more comfortable being with a group of friends and getting to know a boy that way first. Most girls would say that a boy should be a friend first before he becomes anything else.

"Some of my friends who have gone out have felt like they could talk to the person better before they were going out. They felt they were able to be closer before," says Christine.

They didn't like feeling pressure to kiss a boy, or change themselves to be what the boy wanted so the boy would keep liking them. They didn't like feeling that they had to be the perfect person. They decided they just wanted more time to be themselves.

Christine expects that soon enough she'll be ready to start going out with boys. Maybe in eighth grade. Then again, maybe in high school.

She's just going to wait and see.

4

FAMILY

Where Do I Belong

I love my family so much. I am the youngest. Sometimes I get in fights with my sister. She can be a brat sometimes, but I still love her. I love my dad very much. He is really funny and fun. I like to play with him all the time and when we have music on I like to dance with him. He is a good dancer. *ALEX, 10*

I enjoy my family. I just wish me and my family could do more stuff. JENNY, 12

I feel sad when my parents fight. STEPHANIE, 12

I enjoy being alone with my mum. I like it because she understands all my feelings. Sometimes I like going for a walk along the beach with Mum. CAITLIN, 11

SHANNON Age:11

Lives with: her mother, - a weight loss counselor, her father, a coffee salesman, a brother, seven, and sister, nine.

Pets: Smooch, a part golden retriever, part black Lab and part Samoyed, and Fuzzy, a guinea pig that belongs to her brother.

Hobbies: precision skating (large group of girls skating in line together), horseback riding and reading biographies (especially of skaters like Michelle Kwan).

Most embarrassing moment: falling on the ice during a skating session. "I fell and I made a wicked lot of noise and everybody looked at me."

Pet peeve: people eating with their mouths open.

Favorite memory: collecting live sand dollars from a sandbar in the Florida ocean.

I am the oldest in my family. Sometimes I get really aggravated because my parents make me do all the housework that my brother messes. He is seven and he throws trash and I have to pick it up. I live with my mom and dad and I love them. Sometimes I think they are mean and bossy, though. I get into little fights with my little brother. He annoys me a lot. Sometimes I say things I don't mean and then I feel bad. My mom is very loving. She sacrifices for me a lot. She buys me things. She makes dinner and cleans the house and does my laundry. We sometimes argue about stuff like cleaning up around the house. My mom is my friend, my best friend. GINA, 12

I love my family very much. I'm the oldest. I like my family because we talk instead of holding things in. The only problem I have with my family is that my brother and I fight and then talk it out. My mom and I have a healthy relationship because I feel I can tell her anything. SARAH, 12

I am the youngest. My family is a good family. We're average. I don't really have any problems with a family member. My relationship with my brother is weird. Sometimes we get along and sometimes we don't. KAREN, 10

Eleven-year-old Shannon considers her younger sister almost her best friend. Shannon and her nine-year-old sister could have their own separate bedrooms, but they have decided to share a room instead. They like climbing into their twin beds at night and talking to each other in the dark. They talk about school, their friends, the problems they're worried about, and the things they are looking forward to doing.

Shannon realizes her relationship with her sister is special. She's glad she feels so close to a sibling. To have someone to confide in who is sleeping only a few feet away is a comfort. "My sister and I are almost best friends because we just like talking every night. I talk to her more than anyone, except maybe my mom," says Shannon.

The closeness Shannon feels toward her sister is very much the way she feels about her whole family. Her father grew up as one of nine children and his family was always very close. They still are, even as adults, and Shannon's father wants to create that same sort of bond for Shannon and her brother and sister. Every summer, for example, her father's side of the family has a reunion at Shannon's grandmother's house on the beach. It's a time to get together with aunts and uncles and cousins. It is that special season when everyone combs the beach for seashells, relaxes on blankets in the sand together, and enjoys one another's company.

Families come in all sizes and shapes and styles. Some families have two parents married and living together. Some parents live separate lives apart from one another and the children share time with each. Some children have two sets of parents, a mother and stepfather and a father and stepmother. Some girls live with their grandparents or other relatives or, perhaps, some other guardian or caretaker. Some girls are only children, while others have lots of sisters and brothers, or step brothers and stepsisters.

unique

While families are all unique in their own way, the children that are born into those families all arrive in the world needing the very same thing: help and lots of it. When we're born, we are helpless. We can't do anything for ourselves. We have to be fed, clothed and cleaned. We have to be burped and diapered and put to bed. We need love and comfort and caring and we are totally dependent on our parents to provide it for us. But as we grow, something amazing happens. We become more independent. We learn to walk, talk, run. Eventually we learn to recite the alphabet, and later to write it and read it. Through all this, the family's job is to help children to grow to independence; to become strong, healthy, confident and caring adults.

MY FAMILY IS GREAT

My dad always finds time to help me with my homework. Every Thursday afternoon he coaches my soccer team and on Saturdays he takes me to my soccer match. On the weekends he kicks the ball with me. In summer he takes me to the river every day after school for a swim. He is very cuddly. REBECCA, 11

I am the youngest. I have four brothers. My family is cool. I have problems when my brothers hit me. I tell my mom. SHIRLEY, 12

My family is pretty great. My mom and dad are awesome. Sometimes I get in quarrels with them but usually we make up. I have a three-year-old brother. I have sometimes felt that my parents love my brother more than me. I told them how I felt and they explained that was not true. My dad is really great. He tries hard to be a great father. MAGGIE, 11

A time when I was most happy is at Christmas-time. My family gets together and we share so many good memories and friendship with each other. My mom is my best friend. She's not just someone who guides me into right or wrong. She is someone who really loves me for who I am and nothing less or more. VICTORIA, 8

I love my grandma. I help her around the house, clean, carry groceries, and I help her to remember things. After school we do a lot of stuff together. We run errands, I help cook supper and I help her. KEIANA, 8

Mum - our relationship is very close, I can tell her everything and know she won't tell anybody. ANELIESE, 13

Shannon feels really positive about the family she happened to be born into. She enjoys spending time with her family. She loves her parents very much and respects and admires them. They encourage her to do her best, try hard in school, and be responsible. Among the special times they share as a family, Shannon counts eating dinner together on weekends and some week nights when their busy schedules allow it. Because she is a member of a precision-skating team that practices three or four times a week, as many as six hours each week, and she rides horses every Saturday, the family isn't always able to spend a dinner hour together. The meals they do get to share become that much more appreciated, though.

There is a structure to Shannon's family life she has come to depend on. "When I get home, every day my mom always asks, 'How was your day?' We always talk about school projects or what's going on,' says Shannon. She confides in her mother, especially when she has had problems with friends. Once when one friend was ignoring her, she talked it over with her mother. And after hearing what her mother had to say about it, Shannon ended up talking to her friend about things and their relationship is now better again.

"I talk more to my sister and my mom than my friends because I trust them more. You're always going to have your family, but your friends - they can be here today but gone tomorrow. I can tell my mom and sister everything," says Shannon.

She has a good relationship with her father as well, although she says it's different from the ones with her mother and sister.

"I talk to my dad but I can't talk to him about certain things. He's not a girl so he can't understand them as much. He can't understand about how people are nowadays. I can't talk talk to him about other girls because he never was one. He doesn't know what girls look for in each other. Girls are a lot different than boys. They gossip, having hissy fits, but boys just like to punch each other. That's how they are with each other. I can talk to my dad more about sports and stuff. He always tells me school is really important. He wasn't a very good student, he was just average, but he wants me to be a good one. He doesn't want me to do too much sports because it gets in the way of family times. He always says, 'Health, school, sports.' That's the order of things. He's not a big fan of me horseback riding, but I tell him I love being with animals. He loves me doing the skating because it's a real team sport."

MY DAD

I have an extremely good relationship with my dad. I love being with him. He is very fun to hang out with. SHANNON, 11

I am the oldest child because I have a younger brother who is eight. I have had lots of problems with my mum. We row over the silliest things but we always kiss and make up. Although I love my dad, me and mum have a special daughter/mother relationship that I like. EMILY, 12

I also feel sad when I've had a fight with my parents. My family is the best in the world. They are loving, sweet and kind. I have a mum, a dad, and a little sister. I am the oldest child but sometimes I wish I was the youngest. Once I said to my dad, did he like me? and he laughed. But I said I wasn't joking and he said, of course he did. I sat down and told him why. I said because sometimes he ignores me. He said he ignores everybody so I shouldn't worry! I love my family. I have a good relationship with my mum. We can talk about anything. She has a great personality and is always caring. She wears fashionable clothes and helps when you have problems. My mum is firm when she has to be but is the best mum ever! JOLENE, 12

Me and my mum get on very well. I'll do anything for my mum. I love her with all my heart. She is my number-one mum. DONNA, 12

I live with my mom, dad, brother, and sister. My sister is five, my brother is 14, so I'm in between. Sometimes I feel like they gang up on me but I have a really good relationship with my family. I don't have any big problems with my family members but small things tend to annoy me, like my mom, dad, brother, or sister going in my room or using my things without permission. I have a good relationship with everyone in my family. LINDSAY, 12

Mum - she cares for me and looks after me. She loves me. She encourages me with whatever I do. I like going shopping with her. Dad - he loves me. He spends time with me in outside activities. I like when we go fishing together. Also, I like when we make things in the garage. SARAH, 11

The routine of family life that Shannon depends on so much begins each morning when she is up and getting ready for school. Her mother likes to sleep in a little later, so her dad is the one who usually makes her lunch. "My mom always has to add a couple of things because he makes really small lunches," Shannon says.

Beginning the day with a comfortable and familiar routine is important to Shannon. There are patterns of close family life and predictability Shannon enjoys all year round as well. In the summer they go to the beach together. In August, the family rents a cottage on a lake in the country to spend some relaxing and quiet time together. They swim in the lake, take a boat out into the water, and visit the only restaurant in town. Last year, when her skating team competed in San Diego, the whole family went together to the competition. This year, they are traveling to Florida for a competition.

She knows her parents work hard at trying to bring her up right. They impress on her, for example, the importance of honesty. They tell her never to lie because they will find

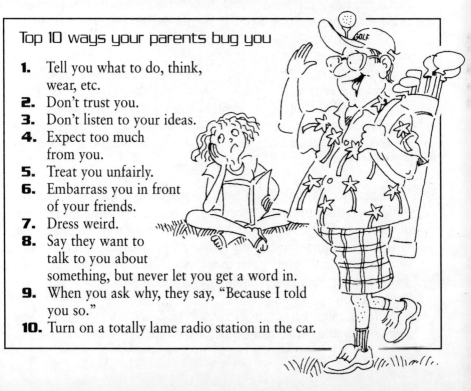

Top 10 ways your parents bug you

1. Tell you what to do, think, wear, etc.
2. Don't trust you.
3. Don't listen to your ideas.
4. Expect too much from you.
5. Treat you unfairly.
6. Embarrass you in front of your friends.
7. Dress weird.
8. Say they want to talk to you about something, but never let you get a word in.
9. When you ask why, they say, "Because I told you so."
10. Turn on a totally lame radio station in the car.

out one way or another. They also tell Shannon she must obey what they ask of her, even if she doesn't agree with them. "My parents are very strict, though if I do what I'm told to do I'm usually okay," says Shannon.

Their biggest conflict so far? Bedtimes.

"If they make me go to bed early, they say, 'We're not trying to hurt you. We are just trying to do what we're supposed to do as parents,' Shannon explains. Still, she has been working to convince them to loosen up a bit about the bedtimes.

"My parents are starting to give in to that. I think they're finally startng to realize I'm older," says Shannon.

My parents can be very fun, but they are also old-fashioned. My mom always puts things off till I'm "older!" My mom doesn't let me do anything that my friends are allowed to do. Like going to the movies when no adult is there. My dad and I are like best friends. MICHELLE, 12

I am an only child. I love my family. They give me a lot of support and know what's going on in my life. They won't let me go some places by myself but I know they just don't want me to do certain things at my age and I respect that. I think that my family could do more things together but sometimes we get busy. But we are always able to have at least one meal together a week where we can talk about our day. I feel I can tell my parents almost everything. ASHLEY, 11

Being the oldest, Shannon feels she has an obligation to set a good example for her younger brother and sister. "My sister and I both like our teachers. We're both good in school. We both really like the same things. She really follows in my footsteps. I don't mind. I look at it as very much of an honor for her to follow in my footsteps. Whenever I do something wrong, my parents say, 'She looks up to you,'" says Shannon.

But Shannon knows that loving her family doesn't mean she always gets along with them. Take her brother, for example. He can

Top 10 ways siblings bug you

1. Read your diary.
2. Use your stuff.
3. Listen in on your telephone calls.
4. Interrupt you at dinner.
5. Hog the TV remote control.
6. Lose the TV remote control.
7. Tattletale.
8. Get more attention from your parents than you do.
9. Do things on purpose just to annoy you.
10. Don't do their share of the household chores.

ARGUMENTS get really annoying. He starts arguments, Shannon says. Or sometimes, he just won't stop talking.

"He just tries to annoy us. He tries to look for attention because me and my sister are together a lot and we don't always include him. I don't know why we don't include him. He's annoying. He's different. My sister and I are both girls. We both skate, we both horseback ride, and he's always butting in about hockey or other stuff. I feel bad we don't include him. We're trying to include him more now because we're getting older. We didn't really realize how we weren't including him before. My mom told us we should try harder to," says Shannon.

One day when the family was at the beach, for example, Shannon and her sister wandered off by themselves, leaving their brother behind. Her mother called the sisters up to the blanket and said they really have to try harder to include their brother in their play. It made Shannon realize they had hurt his feelings.

But as close as Shannon and her sister are, they have had their share of disagreements, too. For example, Shannon is very particular about her bed. It is her own private space and she doesn't really like anyone or anything invading it. "We share the whole room but I tell her to stay off my bed. I don't like having two people on the same small bed," says Shannon.

Although they're not total neat freaks, fortunately, both Shannon and her sister have the same sense of messiness. They both try to keep their room in order, which makes sharing it a little easier. "I don't like it messy, it just drives me nuts!" says Shannon.

But Shannon can have a hissy fit when her sister becomes a tattletale. "If I get mad at her, she's a big tattletale - she'll go and tell my parents." Her other pet peeves about her sister: when she chews with her mouth open and when she does things to annoy her - on purpose!

"She fake cries when I'm doing something wrong. I'll believe she's really crying and I'll say I'm so sorry, then she says, 'I'm just kidding.' Then I get mad," says Shannon.

Can't We Just Get Along?

Were families invented just to drive you nuts? Is your brother making you bonkers? Is your sister more annoying than a persistent mosquito? Are your parents bugging you too? So, the big question is: How well do you get along?

Get Along?

1. It's Saturday, it's been a long week and you want to sleep late. Your mother starts your day with a wake-up call at 7:45, you ...

A. Scream at her, "Give me a break! Even the birds aren't up!"
B. Ask her for just a half-hour more of sleepy peace!
C. Get up, but make her pay for it by being a total grump-head.

2. You're running late for school and your dad is getting annoyed because he's going to drive you. You ...

A. Tell him it's his fault for not waking you up earlier.
B. Apologize for getting up late, and promise to set the alarm earlier.
C. Say you'll just be a minute and ask him to make your lunch.

3. You share a room with your sister and she is the queen of clean. Your attitude is more relaxed about the condition of your room (you don't mind finding your socks under the bed) so you ...

A. Tease her that she's a total neat freak and tell her she should lighten up.
B. Tell her you'll try to keep the common areas of your room picked up, but make it clear that your bed is your kingdom.
C. Tell her what she wants to hear, but hope she ignores the mess.

4. Your brother is so noisy! He's always so loud and bothersome. You ...

A. Tell your brother he's a complete pest and to find someone else to bother.
B. Ignore him or go find a quiet place to get away from him.
C. Ask your parents to soundproof your room.

5. You are planning to host a sleepover with your friends. You want to make sure you have privacy, so you ...

A. Announce no one will be allowed in the living room all night.
B. Ask your family if you and your friends can arrange to have a room to yourselves.
C. Embarrass your siblings in front of your friends so they will stay away.

If you answered mostly As, your family manners need improvement. Try to remember you are not the center of your family universe.

If you answered mostly Bs, you are a sharing, caring family member.

If you answered mostly Cs, you're learning to go along, to get along. Keep trying!

I like my family. They are really nice and friendly. My brother and I are really close. We like to go to places together and do a lot of special fun things. ANGELINA, 12

I feel that my family is very great. I am the youngest in my family. My mother and father are both social workers. My older sister is 14. My family does a lot together and we love spending time with each other. My sister and I get in a lot of fights together but that just brings us closer together. We solve them by simply talking to each other and we learn a lot about one another by doing so. My sister and I have a great relationship with each other. We tell all our secrets to each other and I love her to death. Sometimes I feel like she is my diary. That I can tell her everything. She always understands me and always listens. We have a special relationship. EMILY, 11

When I don't agree with my brother he starts trouble by calling me names and hitting me. I actually argue with him! I'm 12 and he's nine. That's ridiculous. So I solved it by not arguing with him. It was the best idea I could think of. We fight but we have a real close relationship. I stick up for him and he sticks up for me. That's what a family's for. My mother and I are real tight. She teaches me right from wrong. She also teaches me responsibilities. LAKEISHA, 12

I am the youngest in my family. My parents are nice but my sister, 14, is a jerk to me. My sister is mean to me and always makes fun of me. I have to ignore her. LUCIE, 11

I was the saddest when I was alone, no one was home and I had no one to talk to. I'm the oldest and I love it because I get to boss and beat up my younger brother. DEVIN, 12

I am the youngest. My parents live together with me and my older sister. She is 14. It's hard dealing with a teenage sister. Nobody in my family really knows what it's like to be the youngest because none of them are or ever were. They say they do and it makes me really ticked off. My mom is nosy sometimes. She will beat around the bush sometimes to get an answer. Also in a few instances, she has read notes I've written to people. That makes me really mad. My sister is a pretty cool person. She is a good example for me to follow. I enjoy it when we get along. She's just like a friend to me. I can tell her almost anything. JESSIE, 12

Splits, Separations, and New Families

Shannon's parents are happily married and together, but not all parents stay married. They split up for many reasons, mainly because they cannot find any way to get along together and be happy. **It is hard when parents separate**, because the family has changed and change is always a challenge.

Change causes confusion. Children wonder what will happen to me? To my parents? Have I caused this to happen? If my parents no longer love each other, do they still love me?

A family that is breaking up may unleash many strong feelings. Children may feel hurt, anger, and sadness. These are all powerful emotions. So strong, in fact, that the children who are feeling them may not know quite how to express them or to whom. This is especially true if you see that your parents are struggling with feelings of loss and anger themselves. This is truly a stressful time for a family. Many children find it helpful to talk to someone about what they are experiencing, either a trusted adult or even a friend. There are many families who go through such a separation and, after a time, with help and support, gain a new and different stability. The seas may be rocky for a while, but eventually fair weather returns.

I feel saddest when my parents fight. They don't live together any more but they fight on the phone sometimes. I love my family dearly and even my sister. I do have arguments with my family though. I fight a lot with my stepdad but when we're not fighting we get on well. My mum and I are really close. I can tell her anything and she listens even if it's about a friend at school or even school. She's really kind and takes me for who I am. She does everything for me and my family. REBECCA, 11

I was happy when my dad said he was getting remarried. It made me very happy because I loved the person he was going to marry. JACQUELYN, 12

I have an extremely close relationship with my family. My mother is a hard worker, along with my father. I have one older sister who I am fairly close to. My parents separated. They still talk and get along, but of course, it's not the same. I talk a lot with my parents and sister, which helps me a lot. I talk to my mother and tell her almost everything. She tries to do everything for everyone, but being a single parent and having a full-time job - that's extremely hard. ALI, 13

I felt most sad when my mum and dad split up because my dad really hurt me, my brother, and my mum because we love him very much. CHARLOTTE, 11

I have a stepmom, a father, and they have a little girl. My dad also has an older son with a half-mother. I also have a real sister. I have a mother and stepdad. My stepdad has two girls. My two stepsisters are very annoying. I like my other little sister and half-brother. I guess I would be in the middle since I have five siblings. My stepmother ... doesn't feel like a mom at all. ANDREA, 12

Someone Is Missing

Girls are very much connected to their families. It's where they learn how to relate to other people, how to disagree and still love each other, how to share space and get along, how to cooperate and be part of a team. Their deep love and connection to their families goes beyond their parents and siblings. It extends to other relations, as well, such as grandparents, aunts, uncles, and cousins. And the loss of someone in that circle of connections can be a very sad experience indeed.

Many girls say that the times they have felt the most sadness in their lives is when someone they care about and love has been sick or died. This is true for Shannon, too. One summer when Shannon's grandparents were having a house built, it was decided they would move into Shannon's bedroom until the new house was finished. Shannon moved in with her sister, but she didn't mind doubling up in one room, because "I was really happy. My grandparents were really nice and they spoiled us so I was glad they were moving in."

That summer, Shannon was going to camp and the night before her second day at camp, her grandfather fainted. It happened without warning, so no one was prepared for this unexpected event. "We had just celebrated his birthday two days before. He turned 70. We went to a restaurant. We were really happy that we had done that because the day of his birthday, he started to go downhill," Shannon recalls.

"My mom was reading me and my sister a bedtime story and we heard him fall. He was getting Tums to see if that would make him feel better. The ambulance came and my mom rushed us to bed. My dad told us he was going to the hospital."

The next day, Shannon went off to camp as usual, but she was anxious all day and eager to go home and see how her grandfather was. Weird as it was, the bus had a flat tire on the way home from camp and Shannon and all the other campers were stuck there for three hours. "I was really upset because I wanted to see my grandfather. But when I got home, my mom told me he had died ... My mom was really sad, but she didn't want to show it."

I felt the saddest on January 30 and 31. I felt this way because my grandmother had a stroke on January 30 and went into a coma. On January 31, she was pronounced dead. This was very hard for me because she was so dear to me and I loved her so much. Two days after she died, I received a letter in the mail that she had sent me the day before she died. EMILY, 11

I feel saddest when someone really close to me dies. Just last year my great-aunt died. This really upset me because I didn't see her very often and she was really nice. Also when my mum's dad died I hadn't seen him for years, so I didn't even know what he looked like. DONNA, 12

I feel saddest when someone in my family dies. My granddad died on my birthday this year. It upset me a lot. REBECCA, 11

I felt saddest when my grandfather died. I felt sad because I had to realize he wasn't in my life, only in my memory and heart. MAYA, 11

I feel the saddest when a member of my family is injured or sick. A time when I felt like this was when my nanna got very, very sick. I felt very sad because I love her dearly and I really thought, and the doctors thought, that she would die, but she recovered. Thank goodness. ANELIESE, 13

Shannon went to the wake and the funeral. She says one nice thing about it was she got to see her cousins, aunts, and uncles that she doesn't see very often. **Family can be a real comfort at times like those**. The memorial services were a tribute to her grandfather's life. She remembers especially how impressive the 150 policemen were who came on motorcycles to escort her grandfather's coffin to the burial. "My uncle is a cop and my grandfather was very friendly with the police," she recalls. "It was really sad for everyone, but we were happy to see each other because we never get to."

Since that time, her grandmother has moved out of Shannon's house and into her uncle's home, but Shannon and her sister have remained together, sharing the same bedroom, even though they could have their own separate space. "I have the best relationship with my sister. We share a room and enjoy each other's company. We have a lot in common. Like all sisters, we have little arguments.

But...

we've never been a day without having a good laugh, "

says Shannon.

5

SCHOOL

What Am I Learning Here

> *I enjoy school - it's excellent but there are times when I get grumpy or upset.*
> **REBECCA, 11**

" School 1

In school I do my best to get good grades. So far I've been on the honor roll and my parents are proud of me. My homeroom teacher is very understanding. He listens to what you have to say. He cares about people and always listens to both sides of the story. GINA, 12

I love school. All my teachers are very nice and they're smart. (Probably why they're teachers!!) Everyday I can't wait for the next day of school. SHANNON, 11

I hate school!!! My teachers all seem to hate me. But I hate them too. We don't do enough creative writing. We do none in language arts. My teachers single out certain people, so it's really hard for certain kids. My mom understands. She talked to one of the teachers and she has been nicer. JESSIE, 12

I like school because I get to see my friends. My best teacher is my science teacher. He is so funny. Everyone likes him and works hard for him. I find science very interesting. When I'm older I would like to have a job to do with it. JAYNINA, 12

Yes, we do have some problems in school sometimes. We solve them by talking to the people we are having a problem with. Sometimes we ask the teacher for help or sometimes we discuss it with my parents and they will go and talk to the teacher. Sometimes problems just solve themselves. REBECCA, 11

"

EMILY Age: 12 **Lives with:** her mother and father, both professors, and her brother, 11.

Pets: Airdale terrier Max, age one and a half.

Hobbies: reading, acting, running, swimming.

Favorite author: used to be Roald Dahl, but now is E. L. Konigsburg.

Favorite book: used to be Matilda, but now is A View from Saturday.

Pet peeve: her new braces.

Worst moment: "I have a best friend and she moved away in third grade, and in fourth grade I didn't have any friends for a long time. That was a rough year for me."

For 12-year-old Emily, thinking about going to a new middle school for sixth grade made her feel excited. And a little bit nervous. The thing she worried about most was her locker. No more little cubby-holes to store her stuff in. No, this was a **big** deal. She had to find the right locker. Then she had to figure out how to make the lock open, using the right combination of numbers, turning the lock to the right, then to the left. Or maybe it was first to the left and then to the right? Then she had to memorize all those numbers - in the right order, even! Would she ever learn, she wondered.

The panic she felt was enough to make her want to stay in fifth grade. Forever.

But lockers aren't that different to anything else in life, she found out. Emily just had to practice, because, as her mother has told her, practice makes perfect. And, as it turned out, there are things she really likes about having her very own locker, after all.

"We have lockers and I like that a lot better than before. We had kind of like cubbies and at this school you can put whatever you want in your locker. I have a mirror and magnets. We're allowed to put them in there," says Emily.

In this case, Emily not only learned something really important about lockers, she also learned something really important about school. Sometimes the things you think are going to be a big deal, really aren't. And they certainly are not worth staying behind in fifth grade for.

"The first couple of weeks it was really hard. It wasn't hard remembering my combination, it was just hard doing it," says Emily.

And, as Emily discovered, learning to use a locker was only the first of many things that were different about her new school. It seemed to her that everything was different. New students, new halls, new rules, new teachers. She found she had a lot to learn.

"We have different teachers. I like that. Last year, if we didn't like our teachers, we were like stuck with them, but this year, we can switch to different classes."

Emily realizes that we can grow only when we change. This is not always easy, but it's always important. For example, Emily wasn't sure what would happen between her and her old friends once she got to the new middle school. After all, she had been in school with many of the same friends since kindergarten. Imagine! They had learned to read, write cursive, multiply and divide together. Now she was going to be in school with classmates from all over her town, and, the next town, too. What would happen with her old friends? Would they still be her friends? Would she make new friends? Ugggghhh! The whole thing made her think maybe fifth grade wasn't so bad after all.

Tips for going to a new school

♦ If at all possible, try to go to your new school before school starts to learn your way around, try your locker, and find out where your classrooms are. Make sure to look for the places you really need, like the cafeteria, toilets, library, and office. (That is, if you can arrange to do this ahead of time with the principal or headmaster.)

♦ Try not to worry. On the first day, most teachers will be helpful.

♦ Don't be afraid to ask questions. That's how you will get the answers you need.

♦ If you're new to the school and the teacher asks you to tell the class about yourself, here's a suggestion: tell your name, nickname, where you moved from, why you moved, and a hobby.

Best Buds, Forever?

So what happened to Emily and her friends when she went to the new middle school? "I was used to being older than everybody else and now I'm youngest. I was older in my grade and it was different being younger. I didn't mind that change - it was just different. And I definitely changed friends ... I made a lot of new friends and kept my friends from before. They're still my friends. I have more friends than before, that's all," Emily explains.

Emily sits together with her new friends - and old ones - at lunch. "At lunch time, you can choose seats. On the first day of school you choose a seat and sit there until January, and then you choose a different seat until March, and then again until the end of the year. I've changed where I'm sitting, but that's a really big deal for people. I've changed every single time. The popular people have to sit with other popular people. And on the day you pick your seat, you have to come early to get the seat you want, so on that day, everyone's rushing to sit with their friends."

Emily took her time picking friends. She didn't want to rush into anything because picking friends is so important. It is not like choosing what you're going to wear for the day, and changing into a different pair of jeans if you decide you don't like the way the first pair fit. Emily thinks you have to be choosy. "At the beginning of the year, I didn't make many new friends, but then I started to, so I switched to sit with my new friends in January," she says.

The social scene - who sits with whom, who is friends with whom, who is popular - is almost as important as what classes you're taking. That's because for girls, their relationships with their friends, their classmates, and their teachers make a big difference in how they feel about school. It's not just whether they like math or not. It's who's in their math class that's important to girls. And especially, who they sit near.

"Who you sit next to is such a huge deal - especially for the popular people. It says who you are," Emily explains. "When we were

❝ *I like school. With all that's going on at home, it's a way for me to escape. Plus I get to see my friends. ELAINE, 11*

I think school is cool. It is a great time to be with my friends and of course, to learn. JILLIAN, 11

I quite like school because without school you wouldn't have friends. I don't like maths or my teacher. I like my English teacher very much. My other favorite subjects are art, dance, science, English, drama. CLAIRE, 11

I hate school. I know that's where I met most of my friends but I still hate it. I don't like the teachers and I don't like the classes. I HATE math. LINDSAY, 12

My friends and I - like all natural people - get into fights at school. We work them out by writing each other apology notes and sticking them in each other's lockers. EMILY, 11 **❞**

going on an overnight field trip for school, we were on coach buses. And who you sat with was a really big deal. It doesn't matter to me who I sit with, as long as I am with my friends."

School is just about the most important place there is for girls to meet friends and make friends. Maybe you know this already because you're still friends with the girl who shared her snack with you back in kindergarten that day your mother forgot to pack yours. Or perhaps you remember with a smile how your best friend in the whole world saved you a seat on the museum field trip, which made the field trip the best, too! Or it could be that you and your friends in school really help each other out with homework in study hall.

For sure, everything your teacher is teaching in classes is important. But you are learning other lessons in school, too. Like how to be a friend. And who to pick for a friend. How to handle a fight with your friends. And who you can trust. School is the place where girls are getting to know all these things. Or understand them even better.

Girls are really good at figuring out their relationships. They think about them a lot. And this is true of the relationships they have in school, too. Girls are always trying to figure out their relationships with everyone - from the boy that sits behind them in English and always wants to copy their answers to the girl they have to do a science project with and they really don't like. Girls are learning all the time, but they know a lot already, too. Especially about the people in their lives.

Emily says that she thinks the most important thing in making friends is being nice to other people and finding friends who are nice to you.

"If they're nice to me, it doesn't really matter if I'm popular," says Emily. "**Being nice is really important** if you're going to have friends or not. A lot of people say jokes about someone because they think another person will like them, but I think you have to be considerate. To be nice is to not talk about people, especially if they're your friends. I hear a lot of people say mean things about their friends. Sometimes they do that to be friends with other people. But if you're trying to make friends, especially in the beginning of the year, I think that's the most important thing - to be nice. If you see somebody you like, it's important to be nice to them or they're probably not going to be friends with you."

Popular Pals? One thing that was as noticeable to Emily as a new set of braces was how being popular became a really big deal. It seemed to Emily that for a long time, everyone at her school just played with whomever they wanted to. There weren't really any cliques, or secret clubs, or special groups. But that was before. By the time Emily started sixth grade, the scene had begun to change. In a **major** way.

"Popularity" is that kind of weird quality. It's hard to describe, but you know it when you see it. And it can seem like the thing you want most. Girls who are popular seem to be surrounded by friends who are always having fun together. But could looks be deceiving? What makes someone popular anyway? It really depends on the school and the students.

At Emily's school, the popular kids seem to be the ones who have older brothers or sisters. Having an older sibling gives you status, makes you seem older than you really are, she says, and since everyone wants to be older, it makes you popular as well. Even though no one really talks about it, in Emily's school, there are certain things that make someone seem cool.

"Popularity is also based on looks, definitely. Some of the popular people are nice. Some are not so nice. Most of them have certain kinds of clothes, jewelry, or hair. They're in fashion. All the popular people have baggy jeans or certain kinds of shoes and a lot of times they dress alike. If you hang around with the popular people and they like you then, you're popular," Emily explains. "There's always some people who take the lead. Whatever they do, everyone else does too."

Emily says she is not popular, but that it doesn't really bother her.

"I don't really consider people who aren't popular, unpopular. They are just not part of the popular crowd. I don't really care about being popular," she says.

For example, Emily would never choose Spanish over French, just so she could be with certain friends. That happens a lot at her school, but she says that since she can always see her friends after school, she would consider the class first, over friends.

Emily accepts who she is and her place among her peers. However, some girls do feel really miserable because they're not popular. They feel like outsiders, like nobodies. They are unhappy because they don't feel like they "belong." This can be just awful. But no one should have to feel this way for long. It's important to consider just what it means to be popular, anyway. Is this something that's really important, or something you just think is important right at that moment?

I really enjoy being in school. I like being with my teachers. I like them a lot. Sometimes I don't want to come to school, though, because of my peers. My least favorite class is math. Not because of the teacher, because I don't like it. SHANNON, 11

I just moved this year. It's been a big change, but overall I've adjusted. I have excellent teachers which I get along with. The kids are really nice, but I've noticed it's very cliquey here. ALI, 13

I love school, but I don't feel like anyone are my real friends. I have about three real friends in my class. They are only my friends when I have something they like. I don't really hang out with them. LAKEISHA, 12

The different ways people become popular can seem almost silly. They are popular because they wear their hair a certain way? Because they have certain shoes? Or wear a certain kind of jacket? Or like a certain kind of music? To value someone just because of these kinds of things seems just a little bit odd, doesn't it? Instead, shouldn't we value people because they are kind? Caring? Trustworthy? Funny? Aren't these the things we should look for in people? Aren't these the things that should make them popular?

Unpleasant Peers

It is important to find people in your school that make you feel good. The people you spend your time with should make you feel comfortable. They should care about you and your feelings. They should be considerate.

Of course, sometimes people do bug you. Maybe they tease you. Maybe they talk about you. Or maybe they say things to you that make you feel mad, sad, or bad. It may happen to you only once, or it may happen every day. Whatever the situation is, school should be a safe place for you. It should be a place you feel comfortable in. If it isn't, then there's a problem.

Some experts have noticed that girls are reporting more instances of feeling unsafe, bullied, or pressured at school. Sometimes this happens between girls. Sometimes this happens between a girl and a boy. The truth is, it should never happen at all. Most teachers, principals, and parents want your school to be a happy place to learn.

So if you are having a problem with another student and you haven't been able to solve it yourself, **talk to a grownup about it**. If you do not feel comfortable at school, then it will be harder for you to learn all the wonderful and exciting things there are for you to know about.

What to do if you don't feel popular

◆ Try to get involved in activities. Call your friends. Plan to do something. The worst feeling is staying home alone, because it makes you feel even more lonely.

◆ Try to make new friends. Choose friends carefully, not just because you think they're popular. And remember, making good friends takes time.

◆ Choosing a popular person to be friends with is okay, if they are nice.

◆ Be yourself. If you want to become friends with someone who's popular, don't make yourself into someone you are not just to impress that other person.

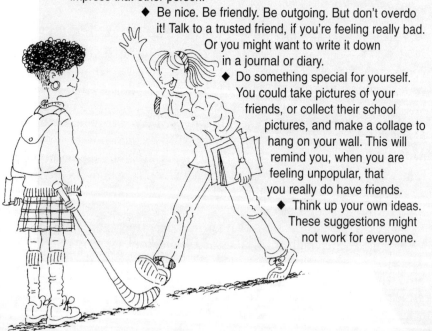

◆ Be nice. Be friendly. Be outgoing. But don't overdo it! Talk to a trusted friend, if you're feeling really bad. Or you might want to write it down in a journal or diary.

◆ Do something special for yourself. You could take pictures of your friends, or collect their school pictures, and make a collage to hang on your wall. This will remind you, when you are feeling unpopular, that you really do have friends.

◆ Think up your own ideas. These suggestions might not work for everyone.

Teachers and Teaching

As you know, every girl is different. Some are tall, or short. Fast or slow. Quiet or noisy. Live with large families or one parent. But the one thing all girls have in common is - school.

Of course, their schools are all different, too. Some girls take a bus to school in a neighborhood on the other side of the city from where they live. Others walk to school a short distance from their home. Their classes may be small or large. They may change classes, or spend the whole day in one room. They may go to a public school with other children from their town or city, or may attend a private school with children from many other places.

But they all have teachers. And probably desks, books, pencils, papers, grades, tests, homework, lunch, recess. All in the hope of learning something useful and important. Parents are children's first teachers. Then come the teachers they meet in school. For girls, teachers are very important because they are the adults they are most connected to in school. Books, classmates, homework are all part of the school experience, but the teacher in the classroom stands heads above in importance.

How to handle problems with people at school

- Talk to them face to face. Ask them why they are doing what they're doing.
- Ignore them. Sometimes this is the best approach.
- Talk to your trusted friends. Ask them for advice.
- If you have a good relationship with a teacher, confide in them.
- If you feel really threatened, talk to your parents, or perhaps a guidance counselor.

I like my school but sometimes the school lunches taste bad. I like all my teachers because I can talk to them. JACQUELYN, 12

I feel that school is just okay. I want to look into private schools to get a better education. My teachers are very nice. One of them is very fat. Everyone makes fun of her and says she is mean, but she is my favorite teacher. EMILY, 11

I sort of like school. Sometimes I like certain classes and sometimes I don't. It's hard sometimes to deal with mean or grumpy teachers but you learn to cooperate and have a good time. ANGELINA, 12

I usually like school. But sometimes we get lots of homework and it gets me stressed out. BRYANNA, 11

I love school! But I hate reading. My teacher always yells when I'm taking a test and I get really aggravated and can't concentrate. MAYA, 11

Of course, there are teachers that are smart, funny, nice, and challenging. If you're lucky, that's whom you'll get. But teachers are human beings, after all, which means that nobody's perfect. You might have a teacher who bothers you in the same way that chalk does when it screeches

across a blackboard. Maybe she always calls on the boys to answer questions and ignores when your hand is waving like a flag in the wind. Maybe your teacher's idea of humor doesn't match up with yours. Maybe she's too quick to give out homework or she always slams her book on the floor to command you to be quiet when she's really mad. Maybe you feel he picks on you, or your best friend. Whatever.

The point is that teachers are a reality in every girl's life. And next to their parents, teachers are the first grown-ups they have to relate to outside of family. So every day, girls are not only getting drilled in spelling or memorizing the periodic table, they are probably also practicing how to deal with a whole new set of grown-ups called teachers.

If you have a problem with your teacher ...

- Talk to your parents, or another adult who will listen to you and perhaps can help.
- Talk to your friends. Maybe they have had problems with the same teacher, too, or another one and have somehow solved the issue.
- Don't give the teacher a reason to have problems with you. Do your work, complete your assignments, get involved with the class, take notes. Maybe you just need to give the teacher a chance.
- Try to figure out what the problem is and ways to work around things.
- Talk to the teacher, if you feel comfortable doing this. Don't be nasty, but express your concerns. Listen to the teacher, as well.
- Just accept the fact that you're not going to love all your teachers. If you are able to pick your seat, maybe sit in the back.

Are You Under Pressure?

Emily says some girls like to be teacher's pets. And everyone knows who they are. But mostly, everyone just does their work. She does think there's a certain amount of pressure on girls to achieve and succeed. She herself feels it.

Some experts worry that **girls are under too much pressure**. That they feel they always have to be nice, smart, pretty. The experts are concerned that girls feel this pressure especially in school. Some studies have shown that teachers tend to tolerate rude behavior from boys, but not from girls, for example. The studies suggest that in some classrooms, two sets of standards apply - one for girls and one for boys.

PERFECT

What does this mean for girls? It could mean that girls are getting the message they have to be perfect! That they should be all-A students, who are dependable, caring, nice, and polite, have loads of friends and plenty of outside activities and achievements. Whew! That's a lot to ask of anyone!

On the one hand, being expected to work hard can encourage you to do so. On the other hand, too many expectations can seem impossible to live up to. What's a girl to do? There are experts who are now concerned that girls and boys should be treated fairly in school. They hope that girls and boys will get an equal education, regardless of ability, interest, background, or hopes. They want **both** girls and boys to be encouraged to work to their best and achieve whatever they're capable of.

"A lot of people want to get all As. I get As in every subject but I get Bs in math. That's my hardest subject. I can get good grades, but I have to work harder in math," says Emily. "If there's a quiz and one person has like a 70 or a C, it makes them feel even worse if everyone has a good grade. We're not really supposed to know what each other gets, but we do because people talk about it. 'He has a D in this class. She gets straight As. I can't believe she has a C in science - it's the easiest class.' Everybody knows - even the teachers know everybody knows."

It's really great that researchers are studying the ways **girls learn differently from boys** and are trying to help teachers to teach better to both. They know already, for example, that girls learn better in groups where they get a chance to talk to each other and cooperate on a project. Boys tend to be more active, hands-on learners. You may have noticed yourself that boys tend to call out more often in class, while girls are generally quieter. This means teachers have to make a special effort to be fair to both. Teachers need to try to use ways of teaching that make sure everybody is learning. This idea is called "gender equity."

Not everyone is an all-A student, though. Everyone has different strengths and weaknesses. That's okay. The important thing is to try to work to the best of your ability. Scientists now think that "intelligence" is much more complicated than they ever thought. Some believe that there are actually seven different kinds of intelligence. Not just one.

The seven ways to be smart are: relating to other people, relating to oneself, and musical, athletic, artistic, logical, and language abilities. It's important to remember this, then: no two people are smart in just the same way!

If you have a problem with a subject ...

- ◆ Try to get extra help on a lesson or chapter that really got to you. When you go for help, be able to tell your teacher specifically where you are getting lost.
- ◆ Ask your peers for help. Maybe they can explain it to you in a way that you'll understand.
- ◆ Ask your parents or siblings for help. Perhaps they can help you understand.
- ◆ Study hard.
- ◆ Accept the fact that perhaps no matter how hard you study, you may never be an A+ student in that subject.
- ◆ Ask your parents to arrange for a tutor, if you really need to go to that extent.
- ◆ Sometimes you can go to a favorite teacher, maybe someone you had last year, for extra help. They know you and understand your learning style.

Like any normal kid, school is definitely not my favorite thing. I'm a good student. Never got detention. I'm always negative about my grades but they come out great. I was the only one with a 100 on my math test out of 68 kids. I don't like my teachers very much. I think we should switch teachers instead of having the same ones two grades in a row. ANDREA, 12

I love school! I am an A and B student. I go to a special class for advanced kids. I love my teacher. She's strict but very fun. My school has a lot of activities and it's really fun. SUKI, 11

I really like school most of the time. My favorite subject is social studies because I have the best teacher. Then I like English because she's a good teacher. Then French. She's okay. Then science, he's pretty bad. Then lastly, math. She's not good at all. In school, material in a class doesn't determine whether I like it or not; the teacher does. DANYA, 14

Well, most people think I'm really smart. My math teacher moved me up in sixth-grade math because she said fifth-grade math was easy for me. I really love history and I get great marks. I hate English and science. MAGGIE, 11

It's easy to see then that school is an exciting and challenging place. It's where girls are learning all kinds of things that will help them now and in their future lives. It's a place where they are learning the math skills, for example, they'll need in order to prepare a business report later on, and it's also the place where they come to understand how to cooperate with other people. It's a laboratory for later life and the workshop of girlhood, right now.

I love school. My class is great. TIFFANY, 8

My friend got accused of cheating. She and the girl next to her had the same answers. But she didn't really cheat. I comforted her until the problem was over. MAGGIE, 11

The classes I like are science because we do other things than work, like, at the moment, we are raising money to adopt a gorilla in my science class. MARIA, 11

I like school. They're not mean teachers. They're young. I call them by their first name. They have a great sense of humor. There are not a lot of people in my classes. I'm studying Spanish, geometry, hieroglyphics, crocheting, and fingerknitting. I like when my classroom is quiet because it's easier to concentrate on doing my work. KEIANA, 8

I like school...

6 DO I THROW LIKE A GIRL?

SPORTS AND OTHER FUN

" *Whenever I ride my bike, afterward I feel good about myself. I am also happy when I spend time with my best friend. I haven't been on any recent teams, but I play basketball, ride my bike all the time, and in the summer, I go swimming because I have a pool. Sports and physical activities are important because you're working your body into shape, because it's healthy, and playing some physical activities can be fun. ANGELA, 11*

I felt most happy when I made it into Majors softball for girls. I felt happy because I would be playing a fun game with my friends. MAYA, 11 "

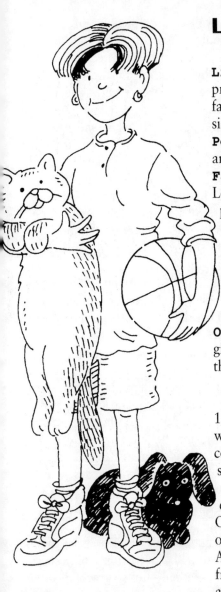

LINDSAY
Age: 12

Lives with: her mother, a preschool teacher; her father, a factory worker; a brother, 14; and a sister, five.

Pets: very big, very furry cat Simba and black lop-ear rabbit Shadow.

Favorite subject: science. Loves to learn about animals and plants.

Favorite pastimes: going to movies with friends, playing outside, going for walks, riding her bike, sleepovers with best buddies, calling friends to come over, and most of all - playing sports.

Outstanding moments: when the girls win a basketball game against the boys at recess.

If you want to get to know 12-year-old Lindsay, just look at the walls of her bedroom. One wall is covered with 50 or 60 photographs she took of her friends. Some photos are from when her class went to an environmental camp for a week. Others are from when they did an overnight camping trip to a pond. And the rest are of Lindsay and her friends hanging out and goofing around. There are also taped up on

I do dance and gymnastics with friends at school in P.E. but I also do play football (soccer) in the garden with my brother sometimes. What I don't like about it is that we have to get changed into gym clothes at school and some of the sports I don't like. I do think some of sports is important because it keeps you fit and healthy. It can also be fun. KAYLEIGH, 11

I do play sports. I play quite a bit of netball (similar to girls' basketball). I used to go to a gymnastic club after school on a Thursday, but I gave that up after I started high school. I now go to a trampoline club which I enjoy. It is brilliant. I do think sports or physical activities are important because they keep you fit and you get to make lots of new friends. Also because it is something for you to enjoy. DONNA, 12

I dance. I have to stand on my tippy-toes. Sports are important because they are good for your body. ROBIN, 9

her wall lots of pictures of animals, including those Lindsay tears out and saves from calendars after the year has gone by. Hung on the wall is a white dry-erase board where every day Lindsay writes a new message reminding herself what she needs to get done or where she needs to be for the day. "So I can remember to do stuff," admits Lindsay. But the most special corner of her room is the one where all her sports mementos hang. There are colorful banners of professional soccer teams and photographs of soccer players she's got autographed. There's one poster of the professional women's basketball team the Lizards, which lists all the players' names, with pictures.

She didn't always love competitive sports the way she does now. In fact, beginning as young as four, she used to love figure skating. She loved lacing up her skates, putting on fancy costumes, and hearing the scraping sound of her blades edging against the ice.

"I did that for five years. I really loved that, but now I really hate it. I just got sick of it. I did it so much, my feet hurt afterwards. It was kind of slow and boring. I like faster things more now. I like to run. I play soccer and basketball - not so graceful stuff," Lindsay explains.

She remembers when she announced to her parents at the dinner table that she didn't want to skate anymore, they were totally surprised. Although skating was becoming less enjoyable, she hadn't really shared her feelings with her parents because she knew they were paying a lot of money for her to skate. She didn't want to complain. But after joining a soccer team, she realized how much more fun playing a team sport was. "I was on a team with all my friends. It was fun all being on a team together," says Lindsay.

If it was the experience of being on a team with friends that first interested Lindsay in soccer, she soon came to enjoy other aspects of playing the sport, too. "**You feel good**, especially when you do something right, especially when you pass or make a goal. You feel, like, good, because you helped. It's like you feel proud ... It's just cool. You know you did it and you can do it again," Lindsay says.

"My coach, he always says he wishes he could give us a shot called confidence. He always wants us to take the ball and go to the basket. If you do it, then it gets easier," says Lindsay. "Once you do it one time, it helps a lot."

Winning women

◆ In addition to being the only woman in the Indy Racing League, the race-car driver Lyn St. James has set 31 speed records in her career.

◆ As an Olympic medalist and all-round competitor, Cara-Beth Burnside has accomplished so much in the mostly male, extreme world of skateboarding that she's the only female with a shoe named after her. It's made by Vans Inc. with her signature inside and her sunburst design on the heel. She appears in the television ads, too!

◆ The champion rock climber Lynn Hill beat many men to the top when she became the first woman - in a single day - to free-climb the nose of El Capitan in the Yosemite Mountains in America.

◆ Women have continued to make significant progress in the World Olympics. In the 1992 Summer Olympics in Barcelona,

34 countries had no women athletes competing at all and women competed in 86 events while men competed in 159. Six years later in Sydney, for the first time women will be competing in the same number of team sports as men.

◆ For much of her competitive career, Karen Burton has been ranked among the top seven marathon swimmers in the world - male and female!

Girls have always been active. They have ridden bikes, jumped rope, played kickball, or competed in volleyball. But now - more than ever before - girls are playing sports and enjoying other activities that they might not have even tried in the past. Some of this change is due to the fact that certain activities simply didn't exist before. When your grandmother was a kid, and maybe even your mother, there weren't skateboards, snowboards, or rollerblades for girls or boys to enjoy. We now have more ways than ever to amuse ourselves and have fun.

The fact that there are more activities to try is not the only reason girls are more active, strong, and lively than at any other time in history. It's also because there's more opportunity and support for girls to play sports and stay active.

Think about it ...

- Professional basketball for women began during YOUR lifetime.
- The Olympics hosted the first women's hockey team games in 1998.
- Worldwide, more than 250 million people play soccer, including 30 million women. In America, for example, more than 18 million people play soccer and nearly 40 percent of them are women. The world is changing fast, and so are the girls and women who live in it. Girls not only rule, they rock-climb, rollerblade, run, and do a zillion other things, too!

I play hockey and I like it because all my friends are in my team and I just like the thrill of the game. I also love music and dancing. I listen to Rage (a music show) every Saturday. I do think sport is important because if you don't exercise you get fat and lazy. Also it is good to be able to play a sport. Sport teaches you to cooperate with others and depend on others.
BROOKE, 11

I do kickboxing every Thursday night and love to run. Also I go swimming once a week because I love it. In my old school I was the second fastest and have been all the way up to year six, but now that I'm in high school, I don't know. I love sports and I will carry on for a long time. I think physical activity is important because it keeps you fit and healthy and in good shape.
SARAH, 12

I feel happy when I go cheerleading and the most happiest time was when we won the Great Britain and European championships at Easter. We won two big trophies and a little cup. I do four sports, which are cheerleading, football, gymnastics, and dancing. I think sports is important because if you don't do sport, you will get fat, but if you do do sport, you will not get fat. CHARLENE, 11

I play soccer and field hockey and I tap-dance. I take jazz too. I play the clarinet and I'm in various music groups at school. I also run to stay in shape. I love to rollerblade and bike ride. I love to move around and I just love to do it. Definitely sports and physical activity is important because you need to stay healthy and stay in shape. The better shape you're in, you'll probably live long and you'll probably be able to fight off diseases like cancer. CHRISTINE, 11

The biggest thing to happen to sports since the invention of the whistle happened in 1972, when the US government made it law that schools had to provide equal opportunity to both girls and boys and Title IX specifically required schools to offer equal access to athletics for girls and boys. Since then, the number of girls playing sports in America has grown amazingly. In 1970, only one out of 24 American girls played sports. By the 1990s, one out of every three girls were playing on a court, in a field, or on an ice rink somewhere. And it's not just in America that more girls are enjoying sports. There is more support for girls becoming active in many other countries, as well.

Lindsay is one of many, many girls enjoying the benefits of all those opportunities and all those changes. Lindsay plays soccer in the spring and each week has two practices and a Saturday game. She also goes to a soccer clinic twice a week to practice her skills. In addition to soccer, Lindsay plays on a basketball team which has games on the weekends and two practices a week. It's hard to juggle all those balls in the air (pun intended). **Sometimes she worries she's not giving enough commitment to each sport**. She wants to keep up her good grades, too. Lindsay thinks her extra effort doing two sports, keeping up with schoolwork, and allowing time to hang with her friends has paid off, though. She feels that playing sports has helped her become more coordinated and stronger. She has more confidence in herself. And who knows where it might lead her in the future? She'd love to play basketball or soccer when she is in college, but doubts that she will ever be accomplished enough to play professionally, although that doesn't take away any of the joy she feels now playing sports.

"At recess, some of the girls who are interested in sports play with the boys who are interested in sports. We play all different kinds of things - sometimes soccer, sometimes football, but mostly we play basketball. Some of the boys aren't as good as some of the girls and some of the girls aren't as good as some of the boys, so we're equal when you think about it like that in that way, I guess," she says.

Five ways to be a team player

♦ Contribute what you can, but remember, no one person can do it all and no one person is a team.

♦ Make a commitment.
Teams take time.

♦ Try your best, work your hardest, but forgive yourself and teammates for mistakes.

♦ There is no I in TEAM.

♦ On the field, friends are teammates and off the field, teammates are friends.

differences

Lindsay says that she sees real differences between the ways boys and girls play sports. When play is rough, girls might get their feelings hurt, especially if someone gets physically hurt in the process of the game. Many girls struggle with the idea that there are winners and losers. They worry about people feeling bad if they lose. And they might also be concerned people will resent them if they win. Competing to be the winner is a new, and not always comfortable, experience for many girls. Learning how to be a teammate is a great new challenge for girls, but definitely worth it, says Lindsay.

> **I dance and play sports. I love it but people get jealous of me because I like to do it in front of people. I don't listen to them, though. That's how I learn to get through tough times. I think sports is important to you and your body. You need to be fit and keep fit. Sports is also a fun game to play. Sports teach you how to be a team player and how it's not important whether you win or lose. LAKEISHA, 12**

I play basketball and I used to do ballet. I enjoy basketball because you can have fun, be in a team, and exercise. I lost my tournament this year in March but we still got a medal. I think sports and exercising are important because kids or elders need exercise, muscles and strength. If you didn't exercise, you wouldn't really be healthy. SUKI, 11

I feel sad when someone on my skating team doesn't try their hardest. I understand if they fall, but I don't like it when they are not focused. I am a figure skater and a horseback rider. I always love going horseback riding because I love the setting with horses. I don't like going skating as much because the setting is cold and boring. There are rewards, though. My skating team and I went to the nationals in San Diego, California, last March.

I think physical activity is very, very important. People who don't do physical activity usually get into boys or drugs because they don't know what to do with their time. Also you would most likely get overweight. SHANNON, 11

"Boys play different than girls play sports. Girls are afraid to do things sometimes. They maybe don't want to make a hard pass. Maybe they're shy. I like playing with the girls but I like playing with the boys, too. Girls are more friendly. If you're having a scrimmage with your team and it's your friend, you might not want to do anything to your friend to hurt her. But boys don't care. If they hurt their friend, they might laugh. They just know it's part of the game. Girls might get mad at each other because somebody got hurt and they kind of think like 'they hit me, she's mean' or 'she doesn't like me anymore.' But boys, they, like, wrestle so they're used to it. Sometimes girls think they might have done it on purpose," says Lindsay.

But mostly playing sports is a way to build new relationships and start new friendships. Or, Lindsay says, deepen old ones. It's a great feeling to be with friends, sweat with friends, and - win or lose - play hard and have fun. She finds that playing sports has been a way for girls to make friends with girls and for girls to make friends with boys, too.

"The boys like to play with the girls because there are a lot of athletic girls in our class. We're all friends - boys and girls. They don't think about us like 'we play with dolls, we wear pink.' They don't even think about that. We just pick teams. They like it. For me, it's different (playing with boys) and I like it. They might like playing with girls for a change, too, because we're not as rough," says Lindsay.

I play netball at school. Sometimes my best position is goal attack because you can shoot and move around the court as well. Out of school I play football with the boys. JAYNINA, 12

During this school year, the girls have played the boys regularly at recess and as the months have gone by, the girls have improved, according to Lindsay. They shoot better, are more aggressive, and make better plays. She says that no one calls them tomboys. To her, tomboys are girls that don't have any girl friends at all, only boy friends. If anything, she thinks the boys respect her more because of her athletic ability.

"**A lot of the boys make fun of girls** that are really girly girls. They don't make fun of the athletic girls because they're more alike. They don't have to make fun of them because they're not so different than them," says Lindsay.

The experts say that girls who play sports or stay active are stronger in every way. They have more physical endurance, more physical strength, better circulation, lung power, and overall are more healthy. They are emotionally stronger too. They feel better about themselves, have more confidence in their own abilities, and believe in themselves. Researchers found that when hundreds of American girls were asked what activity makes them feel better about themselves, the number-one choice was sports! It is interesting to researchers that girls who enjoy physical activities are much less likely to be involved with unhealthy activities and relationships. For example, they are less likely to start smoking cigarettes and more likely to be in a healthy relationship with boys and men. There are many, many benefits to playing sports and staying active. It seems that girls and women who play sports are bound to be winners, but some girls might wonder, "Do I have to play sports? I don't really like organized sports."

The answer is that sports isn't for everybody and you don't have to compete to enjoy the power and strength of your body. Usually everyone enjoys some kind of physical actitivity. So it's important to find something you like doing, and then DO IT! It matters little whether it's playing hopscotch, jumping rope, climbing rocks in your back yard, or chasing your friends, the big thing is to move, enjoy life, find fun or make it. For example, ask your friend to teach you how to skateboard. The benefits?

◆ She'll feel good about showing you something she knows how to do.
◆ You'll feel happy to master some new skill.
◆ You'll both be getting exercise.
◆ You'll be spending time together.
◆ It's fun!

But even with so many things to do, every one of us have been bored at some time or another. It's probably one of the worst feelings in the world. Being bored is like seeing life in only black and white. It's okay, but it could be so much better in color!

Right now, Lindsay is loving life. She has a great family, a solid group of friends she relies on to listen to her, a school she enjoys, many interests and hobbies she pursues, and she has soccer and basketball that continue to challenge her. She hopes some day to get a college athletic scholarship, to be among the growing number of girls who excel as much on the court and field as they do in the classroom. She's not sure a professional athletic career is in her future, but that's okay because she's certain her own happiness is.

What do you want to play?

- basketball
- softball
- baseball
- field hockey
- swimming
- soccer
- gymnastics
- fencing
- dancing
- skiing
- snowboarding
- rollerblading
- skateboarding
- ice skating
- karate

- kickboxing
- boxing
- horseback riding
- archery
- cheerleading
- hockey
- aerobics
- running
- tennis
- track
- water sports
- football
- biking
- volleyball

- badminton
- squash
- racketball
- trapeze
- trampoline
- wrestling
- weightlifting
- rock climbing
- hiking

(In conclusion, there's a lot to do out there!)

Twenty ways to beat boredom

1. Invent a new language.
2. Make a list of all the things you like to do.
3. Explore a place you've never visited in your neighborhood.
4. Call a friend.
5. Make a collage.
6. Take chalk and a yardstick and measure how far you can jump.
7. Check out what the world looks like upside down.
8. Find the shapes of things in the clouds.
9. Paint a picture.
10. Write a poem.
11. Ask your mother to do something with you.
12. Ask your dad to do something with you.
13. Ask your brother or sister to do something with you.
14. Write a letter to your grandmother, grandfather, aunt, uncle, cousin, friend, or pen pal.
15. Organize your closet.
16. Start a scrapbook or a journal.
17. Shoot a roll of film and get it developed.
18. Make a list of what you like about yourself. (It's okay to admit there ARE things you like about yourself.)
19. Make a list of what you'd like to change about yourself. (Be kind to yourself! You should act as if you are your own best friend.)
20. Close your eyes and visualize what you enjoy doing most, then do it.

After school, I do floor hockey in the school gym. I also play soccer and enjoy dancing and singing very much. I think sports and physical activity are both very important. I think that they boost up your self-esteem and it's a great way to meet new people and friends. It keeps you out of trouble and very motivated.
JILLIAN, 11

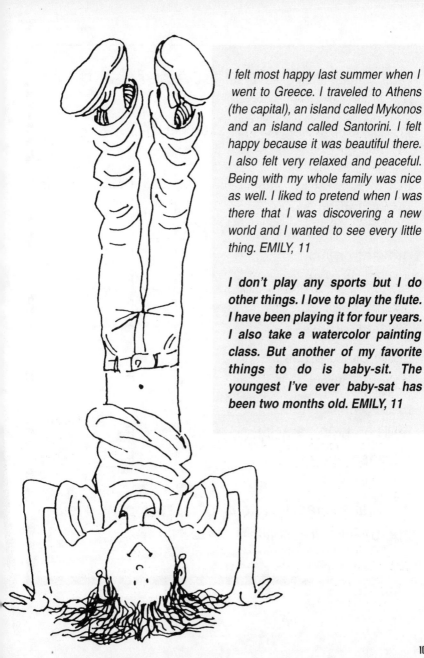

I felt most happy last summer when I went to Greece. I traveled to Athens (the capital), an island called Mykonos and an island called Santorini. I felt happy because it was beautiful there. I also felt very relaxed and peaceful. Being with my whole family was nice as well. I liked to pretend when I was there that I was discovering a new world and I wanted to see every little thing. EMILY, 11

I don't play any sports but I do other things. I love to play the flute. I have been playing it for four years. I also take a watercolor painting class. But another of my favorite things to do is baby-sit. The youngest I've ever baby-sat has been two months old. EMILY, 11

Put yourself to the true-or-false test

Researchers believe that exercise will ...

prevent colon cancer	T___	F___
prevent adult diabetes	T___	F___
prevent weight gain	T___	F___
prevent breast cancer	T___	F___
elevate moods	T___	F___
improve self-esteem	T___	F___
prevent depression	T___	F___
lower blood pressure	T___	F___
improve sleep	T___	F___
reduce anxiety	T___	F___
build up bone density	T___	F___
increase energy	T___	F___

If you answered True to all of these, then you're a true believer in exercise!

7

What Do You See When You Look At Me?

What Do I See?

MY BODY AND SELF-IMAGE

I feel good about my body and I think I look pretty and I feel as though I don't look fat. I have felt uncomfortable about my body when I change for gym. I think someone is going to look and say that I'm fat. I deal with it by changing in front of people that are my friends because I know that they won't say I'm fat. JACQUELYN, 12

I don't think I am really pretty, just okay. I think I am quite nice. I have short brown hair. I am not slim, but not really fat, just a bit chumby (pudgy) on the belly. I have blue eyes. I am quite small. I am not very tall. There have been times when I felt fat and ugly but I just try and forget it. I deal with it by thinking about other people that are bigger than me and I think I am quite lucky. KAYLEIGH, 11

I think I'm okay. I have chin-length brown hair, brown eyes, olive tanned skin, pierced ears, I wear contacts. I have been embarrassed about my body. The skin on my legs is very dry. I use lotion on them every day. It has helped. MICHELLE, 12

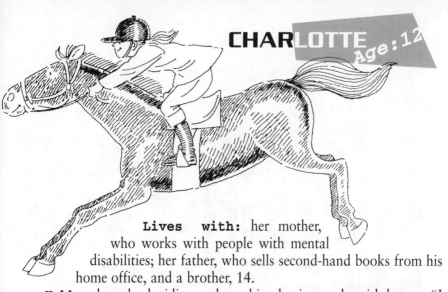

CHARLOTTE Age: 12

Lives with: her mother, who works with people with mental disabilities; her father, who sells second-hand books from his home office, and a brother, 14.

Hobby: horseback riding and anything having to do with horses. "I read Bonnie Bryant horse books. I often look through horse books and pictures in magazines."

> **" I think that everything about my body is proportionate. I would like to have more muscle but otherwise I'm satisfied. I want to be taller, too. As far as weight goes, I don't think I could be any skinnier and be healthy. I could be more muscular, though. When I was younger I was fat. I can't remember a specific incident, but I can remember hating myself because I looked fat. I was always wishing I could look like the other kids. The fact that I got teased didn't help my self-esteem either. Luckily, I've matured and I'm not fat anymore so I'm fine. DANYA, 13**

Right now I'm happy with my body. Sometimes I'm jealous of other people's body parts. I look normal and pretty. I'm Korean. Yes, I've been uncomfortable or embarrassed about my body. I'd deal with it by saying it's no big deal. My breasts are too big and I don't like them. I wear a bra or wear big shirts. Sometimes I'd like to tape them down. MAYA, 11

I feel good about my body. I'm four foot six, blonde hair, blue eyes, glasses. EILEEN, 12 **"**

Favorite music group: Back Street Boys.
Favorite television show: Friends.
Most embarrassing moment: "I was a bit shy when my boyfriend came to watch me ride and I fell off one of the horses. I didn't get hurt really badly - a couple of bruises, that was it."
Pet peeve: "The only thing I really hate is when someone says they're your friend and they talk about you behind your back."

When Charlotte has some time to herself after school or on weekends, she often will spend it looking at teen girl magazines. She might read a story about the Back Street Boys or about the cast of the TV show *Friends* and very often she'll look at the pictures of models. She doesn't always like what she sees.

Her complaint? They're just TOO perfect.

"I just think it's a bit stupid. They only use people who are really skinny. They have to be what they like - perfect. They should put somebody slightly bigger because the models should be like real people instead of stereotypes. They're not perfect to me, but they are perfect to them - really skinny, tiny little hips, big bust, long blonde hair, and blue eyes. Like a blonde bimbo," says Charlotte.

Charlotte isn't the only girl to notice. Many girls have taken note of the fact that every girl they see in the magazines is TOTALLY flawless. She looks awesome! Her hair is perfect, her nose is perfect, even her feet are perfect! It's enough to make you feel like shutting your bedroom door and sliding under your bed forever. I mean, who really looks like that?

Whether girls realize it or not, the images of girls seen in magazines in movies and on television are powerful indeed. Think about it! How many times have you seen a photo in a magazine and thought: I would give away my CD collection to have that ...

... body   ... hair   ... mouth   ... eyes   ... waist
... eyelashes   ... skin   ... smile   ... legs

To tell you the truth, I am not really proud of my body or the way I look because I think I'm fat. When I look at a magazine, all the models are so pretty and thin and I was uncomfortable with that. Then I realized that they don't really look like that. ANGELA, 11

I feel great about my body and the way I look. My parents say that I would be a great model because my body is very strong. I have long brown hair that bleaches itself in the summer, brown eyes, and a size 6 1/2 foot. I am very happy with my body. AMY, 12

I would describe myself as thin, brown/blonde hair - length about to my shoulders, short in height. I think you should not pick a friend because of what they look like. People always tell me I am not this or that. But I would like to tell them it does not matter what you look like, it's what comes from the heart. KIM, 12

Sometimes I can just have one of those days and that could upset me when people criticize me, make fun of me, or tell me I'm ugly. I do my best to ignore it but deep down inside it hurts my feelings. Sometimes I feel great, sometimes I don't. People make fun of my nose and call me Pinoccio. What does it matter? Other times I say, Wow, I'm pretty! It's when people put me down that I have lower self-esteem. I realize that it only matters what I think about myself, not what other people think. GINA, 12

A girl on a glossy magazine cover looking so cool and so totally awesome can give you ideas about the way you should look. Charlotte says she has seen girls do some queer and crazy things to try to perfect themselves - when we all know nobody's perfect! And the pressure to be as pretty as a (magazine) picture doesn't just come from the pages of teen mags or from a movie screen. Sometimes it comes from other girls. The peer pressure of trying to be or be seen in a certain way can make us act in weird and silly ways. Being seen as attractive can seem as valuable as money, and, in the same way that money can make people greedy, wanting to be admired for your looks

can make some people self-centered. Especially if that person doesn't really feel confident in themselves and in all their other qualities.

"I know one girl who thinks she's quite perfect but you still see some faults. She likes people to think she is perfect, but she knows she isn't really," explains Charlotte. "She likes people to think she is going to be a model. She says, 'I'm going to be a model, but you couldn't. You don't have the right nose. I've got the right body. You don't have high enough cheekbones, but I do.'

"She has brown hair, layered into a perfect hairstyle, and she thinks it's really brilliant. She's quite skinny. I don't think she's very pretty but she thinks she is. The people I talk to think she's pretty stupid, she's just showing off. A few of them treat her like a queen. 'Stand back, here she comes. I can't talk to you, she's coming! I have to talk to her.' She doesn't really like those friends, she just uses them because she knows they think she's brilliant. She uses them when she needs something - just to be a show-off, to say, 'I've got so many friends.' I think they can't find many friends and so they can say, 'Look, I'm friends with her.' When they're apart from her, they're really nice, but when they're with her, they tend to be like zombies. They follow her all the time and do whatever she wants. She'll say, 'Go and buy me this from the shops' and so they have to do it or otherwise she won't be their friend."

So looks - everything from what clothes you wear to your waist size - can be tremendously important to girls and have a huge impact on their relationships with other girls. Some girls become popular because they're cute or pretty or dress in the latest styles.

But all in all, looks are only skin-deep. It's the girl underneath the surface of those looks that really matters.

Meet Jordan Johnson

At the age of four, Jordan Johnson already knew the thrill of a beauty pageant and the excitement of the wave and smile before an adoring audience. Now nine years old and weighing a mere 50 pounds, she also enjoys the wallop of the wrestling mat.

She's been wrestling against boys and girls for two years as a member of USA Wrestling. In a wrestling match, size is not important - weight is. So Jordan wrestles against other boys and girls the same age and weight.

"I just thought wrestling might look kind of cool to do and I wanted to see what it was like and it was fun," says Jordan.

Now Jordan sees herself as both strong, and beautiful.

Her coach Jay Roman says Jordan has the mental toughness wrestling requires, as well as the physical stamina and strength. "I put her near the top in terms of mental toughness. She holds up just as well as, or better than, any of the boys do. Some kids have the mental makeup to be a wrestler and I don't think it matters whether it's a boy or girl. Girls might be a little less confident than boys starting out, but with encouragement, quickly become as confident."

So what do girls do to be beautiful?

They cut bangs and pluck brows and pick zits and paint nails. They spend a lot of time in front of the mirror and a lot of money at the mall. Think about it - the cosmetics industry is a $22 billion business every year, just in the United States! That's a **lot** of mascara, blusher, eye shadow, lip gloss, moisturizer, body wash, perfume, etc. For sure, girls get the message early in life that they should be both nice **and** pretty. Research has shown that girls get a lot of praise and attention for their appearance and so get the idea that being a girl means being attractive.

Is that good or bad?

It's probably both.

Girls should be encouraged to look their best and feel good about themselves. The problem is when there is SO much emphasis on appearance, some girls get the idea that image is **the most important thing**, which is not good. Consider what happens when girls start thinking that if skinny is good, then skinnier is better ... They weigh themselves and then waste their lunches. They worry and watch, measure and match. They compare and contrast every little thing about themselves to everyone else in the world! Some girls starve themselves, skipping meals to lose weight. They become obsessed about their size. This is very risky.

Charlotte's mother has worked with girls who have got themselves into trouble by starving themselves to skinniness. It's unhealthy and dangerous. "I've seen them on videos or pictures of them and they're **really skinny**, but they still think they're fat," says Charlotte.

unhealthy

Charlotte has seen girls at her school that also seem to be worried all the time about their weight. She thinks these girls haven't really accepted their own bodies, whatever their size and shape.

"Quite a few girls in my class say, 'I'm not skinny.' Most of them are the skinniest in the class, but they think they have to be better. They think, If I'm not lighter tomorrow, then no one is going to like me. I have to go on a diet really quick. Some girls come in and don't eat anything. They say, 'You can have my lunch, I'm not having any lunch.' And they're not eating

I feel fat and I don't think I look nice. I always feel self-conscious and ugly, even if people say I'm not. I always feel uncomfy! I'm embarrassed about my size and things like that. I always think people are laughing at me, but sometimes I think I look alright. VICTORIA, 12

any breakfast or any dinner," says Charlotte.

Then there are the girls who are overweight and worried about that.

"They lie about their weight. They wear clothes that are really too tight and say, '**Look, I'm only this size**.' I see all these girls around being really stupid. They just look silly when they say, 'I'm not going to eat.' I'd rather eat healthily and keep fit, rather than eating a lot and saying I have to go on a diet."

Charlotte realizes it's really a challenge to learn to accept your body. Sometimes there are things about your body and your appearance you can change as quickly as a new haircut. But there are other things you are just born with that are as fixed as freckles. Charlotte had to learn to like her height - which has not always been easy.

"I'm quite short," she confesses. "I don't like being short because everyone is taller than me. I'm just under five feet. I'm a bit aware of being short when we're at school and they're four or five inches taller than me. There are a few people even smaller than I am so I don't feel too bad about it. I think some taller people would accept me as their friend. I think they're embarrassed being around shorter people. All the tall people seem to stick with the taller people. I

I feel okay. I'm working on playing hard and not giving up. I'm kind of skinny but wish I could be less. I have blonde hair and am four foot eleven. I was embarrassed by my feet. They are very big and so I just ignored them. JENNY, 12

I think I'm pretty. Not drop-dead gorgeous. I'm very skinny and lightweight. Sometimes I wish I were normal. My mom's on a diet and she puts the whole family on it. I tell my mom I don't like it but she doesn't listen. ELAINE, 11

I am medium height with dark hair, dark eyes, olive skin, and I am a medium build. I feel okay with my body but my legs and bum are a bit fat and chubby. BROOKE, 11

think they look a bit funny at the smaller people. The tall people say, 'Oh, you're so small and cute!' You don't want to be thought of as small and cute, you want to be thought of as tall like them. But then, some of the tall people say, 'I wish I was small like you.'

Who Am I?

My breasts are getting bigger. New hair is growing in weird places. My skin is erupting. My hips are wider. My face looks different. I'm getting taller.

I don't recognize myself.

Sometimes I feel like a total freak. It's a little bit scary and takes some getting used to. I hope I can.

So...

the real deal on growing up is this: your body is going to change. Duh! So get real and get down with it. It may happen slowly over time; then again, it may seem to happen overnight. One minute your face is clear as a summer night in the country - the next it's pimple city. It can feel downright creepy to have your body seem out of your control.

What to do?

♦ Learn what you can about what is happening to your body. Hormones shouldn't be a mystery, because, after all, mysteries can be scary!

♦ Talk to your closest friends about your concerns. They are probably wondering about the same things you are, and maybe worrying about them, too.

♦ Confide in a parent, older sister, or other trusted adult like a coach, about your questions.

The goal is to grow up and to feel comfortable about it. It's that simple. You want to accept yourself - no, wait - actually like yourself in the process.

"Girls I know that have big boobs and wide hips hate them. 'I wish I was undeveloped,' they say. One of my friends, she's a bit funny about her hips. The clothes won't go over her hips. When she bought clothes when she was younger, they were easy to pull up. She finds this a bit annoying. She seems a bit older than she looks. It's because she's grown up a bit faster than us. The rest of us are still in the middle of what's happening to us. I go to her for help with things. I go to her for advice. Normally I ask her about feelings and mood swings and things. She know what it's like," says Charlotte.

"I do have a friend who is 16 and she helps me out quite a bit. Her body started to change - not really, just a little bit, I suppose. It's really hush-hush at our school. If you do start developing you're really like a strange weirdo. When you're in a younger year, it's not right. When you're in an older year, it's normal."

When a girl gets dressed in the morning, chances are she looks in the mirror and thinks to herself:

1. How do I look?

2. What will my friends think of how I look?

3. What will the boys think of how I look?

Boys are a fact of life. They're there at the bus stop, on the playground, in the classroom. In fact, they're everywhere. And their very presence can put pressure on girls in a whole different way. It can be flattering to have their attention. Girls may feel like they have to look a certain way to appeal to boys. They might think, I have to be pretty for boys to like me. Then again, they might not.

The important thing is for girls to feel comfortable about themselves in whatever company they keep. Girls need to feel free to

be themselves – not try to

make themselves over into something else entirely. Think about this: makeup should enhance your looks, not cover up the real you! In other words, it's okay to make the most of your appearance, just don't try to make it over entirely.

SELF-ACCEPTANCE

I felt uncomfortable about my body when I started developing breasts. I felt embarrassed when I learned about menstruation and puberty. I got embarrassed also because the boys joke about PMS. I learned to deal with it because the boys are going through changes too and it's not a private thing. LAKEISHA, 12

1. When I am having a bad hair day ...

A. I pretend I am sick so I don't have to go to school.
B. I wash my hair again and start styling it all over until it's perfect.
C. I laugh about it with my friends.

2. It's the hottest day of the year outside and I ...

A. Wear something long to hide my thighs.
B. Wear short shorts to show off my legs.
C. Wear shorts because I don't want to melt in the heat.

3. All my friends want to spend a day at the beach, but I've just gained five pounds ...

A. I make up some excuse why I can't go with them.
B. I go, but I wear regular clothes - even though I feel like a dork.
C. I pull out the bathing suit I feel most comfortable in, but just in case throw on a T-shirt too.

4. A boy at school calls me Shorty all the time ...

A. I tell him, "That's better than being a BIG jerk!"
B. I ignore him until I get home and can have a good cry to myself.
C. I say, "That's okay. Great things come in small packages."

5. All my friends have cute little feet and I have size 10 ...

A. I always hide my feet under my seat at school and hope that no one notices their gargantuan size.
B. I try to find shoes that make my feet look smaller.
C. I decide, who cares? I give myself a pedicure.

If you chose three or more A answers, you could give yourself a few more hugs each day. Don't be so hard on yourself!

If you chose three or more B answers, you are well on your way to becoming your own best bud.

If you chose three or more C answers, you owe yourself applause because you accept yourself **and** respect yourself.

Charlotte follows the example of her mother, she says. "My mum doesn't care what other people think. As long as she likes it, she's happy - which is a better way. As long as she's happy, that's what's important." So Charlotte's mother usually only uses makeup for a special occasion, like a wedding or a party. But even on those special days, she doesn't use "anything that's going to change the way she looks," Charlotte says.

Charlotte has seen the disappointing results of some makeup attempts among the girls she knows. Too much mascara here, too much eye shadow there can be the beginning of a real makeup disaster. Charlotte says, "A few of my friends don't think it looks very good when you're young and you use makeup. I think you should use it when you're older. It just looks silly - all smudges around the eyes, lipstick all over, eye shadow right up to their eyebrows. They don't know how to do it. They think it makes them look older and really cool but it looks really silly - like you have a black eye or something. Most boys prefer you naturally, without any makeup."

I'm average. Normal. All that kind of stuff. I used to think I was fat. Now, all these boys like me and stuff. It has boosted my self-esteem. JESSIE, 12

Most boys say that I am fit and pretty and I get all shy. My friends say I am pretty. REBEKAH, 11

In other words, sometimes less is more. And always, accepting yourself is best!

It's a Barbie Thing

Girls have been playing with Barbies for more than 35 years. They have been styling her hair, changing her clothes, and putting spike heels on her teeny, tippy-toed feet for ages. Talk about being popular - Barbie is so popular that there have been enough Barbies made to fit around the planet three and a half times! Think of it: a billion Barbies! She's the most popular toy **in the world**. Two Barbies are bought every single second of the day, every day, all year long. The average American girl owns eight Barbies, the average German girl seven, and the average girl in Italy or France owns five.

So what is it about Barbie that makes girls want to blow their allowance on **one more outfit**, or beg their parents for the latest Barbie? Is it her hair? Her clothes? Ken?

It's probably all that, not to mention that Barbie is just fun. It's amusing to imagine life as Baywatch Barbie with her jet ski and windsurfer and - don't forget - her dolphin pal. But consider this: if Barbie were a real live person, with her bust to waist to hip size, she probably couldn't stand up. She'd most likely topple over, unable to hold herself upright.

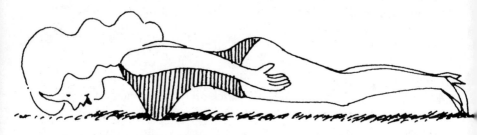

The Body Shop, a company in England which sells a line of herbal and natural body-care products around the globe, is concerned about Barbie's image and what it suggests to girls. The Body Shop founder Anita Roddick and the people at the Body Shop worry that Barbie gives girls the idea that they need to grow up with a huge bust, barely any waist, and feet that won't lie flat! Anita wants to keep fact and fantasy straight for girls, and her company is now popularizing a different image - a definitely-not-Barbie doll called Ruby. She is pretty, but also not perfect. Like the Body Shop says, "There are 3 billion women who don't look like supermodels and only eight who do."

Whether girls are tall, small, wide or narrow, brunette or blonde, freckled or fair, is not as important as it is how they feel about themselves. If your best friend was feeling frumpy and grumpy because she was having a bad hair day, you'd probably tell her not to worry. 'You look fine,' you'd say. You would reassure her. You might help her fix her hair, or make a joke about it, or otherwise make her feel comfortable about her appearance. In the same way, having a strong self-image and positive self-esteem means **being your own best friend!** Everyone has an off day when they're unhappy with their looks, but you have to act to yourself as you would to your best friend and say, 'It's okay. Get over it!' You have to believe in yourself, because if you don't, who will?

Sometimes girls get bothered and bummed out because they feel they are not like anybody else. The truth is: **we are all diferent**. And that's great! We don't have to be like anybody else because we are unique. We're imperfect and interesting at the same time.

"I don't think anything is perfect. No one is going to be perfect. Everyone can be special in their own way. No one is better than any of you. Even if you've got something really nice about you, you've got your faults, as well. There is no perfect me," says Charlotte.

I'm happy about my body. I'm pretty. I wear sneakers a lot. I have brown eyes. I usually have my hair braided. I'm African-American. I'm tall. I'm chunky.
KEIANA, 8

I don't want to sound conceited but I think I'm very pretty. I love the way I look and I'm not going to change it. I love my body and I'm not embarrassed by it.
SHANNON, 11

I think I am small at four feet six and a half inches, but I like being small because I always get to be in the front in dancing and people can see me. I am pretty skinny with a few rolls here and there, but overall I think I am pretty fit for weighing 75 pounds. I wouldn't want to weigh less because I would be too skinny but I don't have the perfect body. ASHLEY, 11

8

THE
FUTURE

"

I think I'll be a teacher or a vet when I grow up. I think I'll be happy. KATE, 12

I want to be famous. I like to act or I like to do sports. But I would like the world to know about me. I also would like to do something that would help the world. BRYANNA, 11

I don't know what I want to do when I'm older. I just want to enjoy my life while I'm young enough but when I do get a job, I'll make sure I'll be happy. CHARLOTTE, 12

In my future I will be a doctor and a first woman president. SARAH, 12

I see myself being an architect or interior designer, with a husband, children, and a nice house. And yes, I will be happy. ANELIESE, 13

"

EMILY Age: 11

Lives with: her mother and father, both social workers, and sister, 14.

Favorite book: The Devil's Arithmetic.

Worst moment: "My sister and I went to this camp. We did a play and I had a really big part. It was a singing solo. I was practicing and practicing. When it came time for the play, I just totally forgot everything ...We have it on tape."

Favorite poet: Langston Hughes.

Favorite book of poetry: The Dream Catcher.

Favorite author: Jane Yolen.

Pets: a nine-year-old golden retriever named Cookie, a parakeet called Picky Picky, a very fat barn cat named Toby, and a money cat, Patches, that was a stray.

Most annoyed by: braces. "I have to wear braces, I have to wear headgear and I have to go the orthodontist's office."

Accomplishments include: reading her first book at age four and writing cursive in first grade.

When I get older I hope I will be a lawyer or pediatrician. I have high expectations for myself because I know I can be great. I know that I'll be happy in what I do whether I am a lawyer, doctor, mother, teacher, or secretary. I'm excited to grow up. DANYA, 13

I will be really outgoing and have a gorgeous boyfriend, preferably David. SARAH, 12

I would like to be an actor, a zoo person (I like animals but I wouldn't want to be a vet because you have to see heaps of blood and I don't really like that), and a model as well, but I don't know if I will be. I think I will be happy. CAITLIN, 10

I see myself being an air hostess or a cruise hostess and traveling to a lot of different places. I will be even more happy if I have kids and live in a small town. BROOKE, 11

Emily does it all. At age 11, she's tried so many different things. She's written books of poetry, performed flute before large audiences, taken fabulous photographs, and baby-sat for children as young as two months old. She says that when she grows up she'd like to be a poet, flutist, photographer, and artist. Oh yeah, and a mother, too! So basically, the way she sees it, Emily has spent much of the first 11 years of her life getting ready for the rest of it.

"I've been able to do so many different things, but I love it!" says Emily, who also spends her time doing art and reading. She plans to start basketball, too.

Emily is excited about her life. She feels **really** lucky to be who she is and living with the family she does. She loves her parents very much and appreciates all that they do for her. She especially feels fortunate that they have encouraged her to try so many different pastimes and hobbies and experience the world in so many different ways. She also loves her older sister. Believe it or not, they might fight sometimes, but she considers her sister a real-life role model.

Emily is not only smart, she is pretty wise for her 11 years. Like other girls, she has a lot of insight into her life. She can see already, for example, that the things she is doing now, or has done, are helping her prepare for whatever else she does with the rest of her life - whether it's playing with dolls or practicing the flute.

"I was one year old when I got my first doll. My sister and I would play for hours, dressing up our dolls. Then we'd take them out. We'd practice how to change diapers, how to hold them right, take them in the carriage," says Emily.

Playing with dolls naturally led Emily to playing with real-life children. As she got older, she met other children younger than she was through her mother and her mother's friends. She enjoyed spending time with them. She liked to color with them, play games with them, or play house with them. All those experiences helped her when she was finally old enough to baby-sit.

"I've baby-sat a two-month-old baby, but I felt really comfortable. I was confident because I've had so much practice. My mom thinks I'd be really good doing something with kids - a pediatrician or a social worker with kids or a teacher. I know a lot of people older than me have no idea what to do in an emergency," says Emily.

I can see myself being either a vet or a window dresser in Harrods or a nursery teacher. I really think I will be happy.
CLAIRE, 11

In my future I believe I will become a person that is involved with fashion. I love doing hair and modeling. That is what I'm expecting to be in the future.
SUKI, 11

I think I'll be a newscaster because I love to talk.
DEVIN, 12

I see myself as an architect. I would be happy because I love to draw and measure. So I t hink I would enjoy this. Also because I love to look at houses. The reason I think about my future is because I want to make it just right. KIM, 12

I will be married and be playing with my kids.
JESSICA, 9

"When I was baby-sitting this little baby, she was six months old and she rolled off the couch and hit her head. Most people would be all scared and get all panicked and that would make the baby more upset. So I was really calm. I just called my mom. Just knowing what to do really helps make you more confident and not scare yourself."

A child's play is an adult's work.
Really!

Take playing with dolls, for example. Just like Emily, many girls get lots of practice pretending to take care of dolls before they take care of real-life babies. They tuck them into cribs, rub their backs and burp them, hug them and kiss them - all the things they'll probably do with a real baby later on, or, if they baby-sit or have a younger baby in the family, they might be doing already. That way, you can make mistakes and learn from them, which is much safer for the baby - for sure! If you drop a doll in the tub, it's no big deal, right? If you diaper a doll backwards, so what?

If you leave a doll outside to bake in the sun wearing her best winter coat, it doesn't really matter all that much.

"When I was little, I definitely thought I was going to be a teacher. I'd line up all my dolls and take a picture book and show them the pictures and read to them. Or I'd cook for them or take them out for walks. I'd even take three of them with me to the mall. I'd take a carriage and all these diaper bags. People would be like, 'Oh, she's so cute!'

Well, lots of things girls play and do are the same as playing with dolls. They're the things girls learn from, and they're the things that help them prepare for the big wide world of being a grown-up. Because dolls are a common plaything for girls, many grow up to take on jobs that require them to take care of people or have strong skills working with, talking with, and relating to people. Lots of experiences girls have when they're young are introducing them to jobs they might consider when they're adults.

Take Emily, for example. If she had never taken a flute lesson, she might never know that she'd like some day to be a professional flutist, maybe playing in an orchestra or on stage. And what in the world ever made her pick up an instrument that looks like a silver stick with lots of holes in the first place? That's just the point - she didn't! First she tried piano.

"I think if it hadn't happened that way, I might not have taken an instrument. My parents have really introduced me. When I heard my mom playing piano, then I wanted to play piano. So I took piano lessons for a while," Emily recalls. Not only did her mother have an interest in music that helped spark hers; her dad also did. He used to play the saxophone. They both encouraged her to try to play a musical instrument. At first she liked the piano, but then decided to make the switch to a smaller, more portable instrument. In other words: the flute.

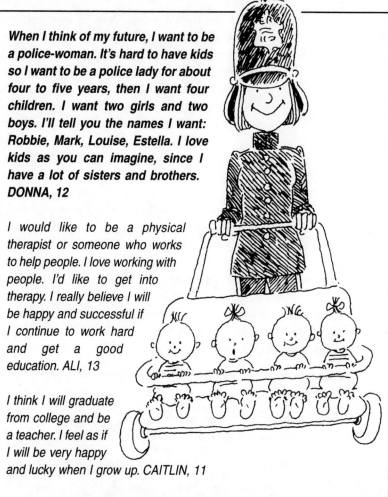

When I think of my future, I want to be a police-woman. It's hard to have kids so I want to be a police lady for about four to five years, then I want four children. I want two girls and two boys. I'll tell you the names I want: Robbie, Mark, Louise, Estella. I love kids as you can imagine, since I have a lot of sisters and brothers. DONNA, 12

I would like to be a physical therapist or someone who works to help people. I love working with people. I'd like to get into therapy. I really believe I will be happy and successful if I continue to work hard and get a good education. ALI, 13

I think I will graduate from college and be a teacher. I feel as if I will be very happy and lucky when I grow up. CAITLIN, 11

I want to be a nurse or a doctor because I rub my grandma's head a lot when she has a headache and she says that I have healing hands. Yes, I will be happy. KEIANA, 8

Emily practices the flute five days a week, between 15 minutes and half an hour each day. She plays in school with the school band as well. But mastering the flute isn't just a matter of figuring out all that fingerwork. It's a mind matter, too. Emily knows that to be good at playing flute, the right *attitude* attitude is as important as reading the right page of music. For Emily, that means making a commitment and sticking to it. It means challenging herself, and it also means enjoying herself. She feels happy and pleased with herself when she tries hard, works hard, and plays well.

"Sometimes I imagine myself getting better and better and making a tape some day. My teacher assigns me music pieces each week and I want to conquer them. I want to add to it, take it and make it my own," Emily explains. "I think it's going to help me later on. I might want to have a career as an instrumentalist or maybe as a painter."

I think about my future a lot. I want to be a dolphin marine biologist. I love dolphins. I'm comfortable with the ocean. I think I will be very happy doing that. SHANNON, 11

I see myself playing pro soccer and going to the World Cup. Yes I'll be very happy. CHRISTINE, 11

I think about my future a lot. I see myself as a professional football player. I will be very happy because I'll be famous. JACQUELYN, 12

In the future I hope I don't get fat. I would like to be a public accountant or something like that. KAYLEIGH, 11

I'm going to be a dolphin trainer and it will be wicked fun. ANDREA, 12

With my future, I see myself as a P.E. teacher or a dance teacher and feel I will be very happy doing this. KELLY, 12

There was a time when girls didn't have many choices about their future. They might be a teacher; or a nurse; or a secretary. And most every girl grew up to get married and be a mother. That was pretty much it. But since the 1960s and 1970s, women have been demanding to have all the same choices about their lives as men do. They can be construction workers or cops. They might be a pile driver or a dentist. They could choose to be president or a parent, or both!

Yet, with so many choices, how do you know what to do, where to begin, who to be? Girls are facing a choice that their grandmothers generally never had to make. Do I have a career? A family? Or can I do both?

Two thirds of all mothers with children younger than school age are working. Three quarters of women with children that are in school are working. That means that the majority of women have made the decision to do both: be a parent who also works outside the home. Maybe this idea isn't on your brain scan right now, but it might be something you have to consider at some point. And there is no right or wrong answer. There are no easy answers, either.

What is totally weird, though, is to realize that the experiences you're having now - even right at this very moment reading this book - are influencing what you'll be doing 10, 20 or 30 years from now. You may have borrowed a biography on Amelia Earhart from the library and decided flying is the life for you. You may be swimming for fun in the summer and realize that being a lifeguard would be a really cool job to have poolside. Perhaps you join the drama club at school and are suddenly inspired to a life on stage. Emily knows that even if you're just playing, you're practicing. And that's the best way to decide what you like or don't like.

What job would suit you?

Are you outgoing?
Enjoy talking to people?
Then you might be a flight attendant, a waitress, or a telephone operator.

Do you like doing people's hair?
Enjoy painting your nails?
Then be a hairstylist or manicurist.

Do you like to show people what you know how to do?
Are you always the teacher when you play school?
Then you're a natural-born educator.

Do you love booting up the computer and getting into a challenging program?
Would you find life boring if computers were zapped from the face of the earth?
Then your career might be at a keyboard.

Does science thrill you?
Are you fascinated by bugs? plants? pets? bones and blood?
Then you've been bitten by the science bug.

Do you like to play store?
Run a cash register?
Then you might be happy working in a retail store.

Are you argumentative?
Do you like taking a stand? Asking questions? Getting answers?
Then you should consider becoming a lawyer.

Do you keep your secrets in a journal?
Is writing the way you best express yourself?
Then writing for a living might make you happy.

Does a paintbrush in your hand feel like an extension of your body?
Do you like to express yourself with images, rather than words?
Then you have the soul of an artist.

Does music move you?
Do you hear a piece of music and it stays with you forever?
Then you might write music, play in a band, or work in a recording studio.

Is religion really important to you?
Do you wonder about God? The all-powerful? Jehovah? Buddha? Allah?
Then perhaps you have a holy calling.

Do you think you would like to heal people?
Does the science of biology interest you?
Then you might make a fine doctor, nurse, or x-ray technician.

Are you always imagining what life would be like if you were a different character?
Are you a dramatic-type person? Do you enjoy being the center of attention?
Then you should consider a life in the footlights of the stage.

Do you like taking photographs?
Recording the family birthday parties on videotape?
Then get a camera quick!

Do you like to be in charge?
Are you industrious?
Then there's a business out there waiting to be started by you.

"I really like poetry. It's a way to get your feelings out. Photography - I like capturing different things. Kids - I really enjoy. I'm looking forward to being a mother. I really like kids a lot," Emily says.

At age eight, about the same time she started taking flute lessons, Emily also started writing poetry. Her parents had given her a book when she was four or five on how to write poetry. And by the time she turned eight, she was making up little books of poetry. Again, just like with the flute, she was encouraged by her parents to take up something new and try it for herself. That kind of encouragement and support by parents, or teachers, or coaches, or siblings, is very helpful in building confidence for the future.

"I'm a pretty good student. I get straight As. My dad helps me in math. My mom helps me in other stuff. I owe a lot of it to my parents for teaching me early on. I could write in cursive in first grade when everyone else learned cursive in third grade. If I just did the regular criteria, I wouldn't learn as much. I really try to go the extra mile. I think that it was my second-grade teacher who got me to see that - to put the extra effort in, not just do certain things. In work, in my career, I think I will always try to do more, be better than I think I can. I can go a step further," says Emily.

With such a demanding schedule - flute practice, art lessons, schoolwork and baby-sitting Emily has had to figure out how to manage her time. It has meant she's had to decide what's most important to her. She hasn't had a lot of spare time to devote to sports, for example, although recently she's decided she's going to start playing basketball. At her parents' insistence, she also doesn't watch television during the week - weekends only. And her parents require her to read 12 newspaper articles for every hour of television she watches. "Each article equals five minutes of television," says Emily.

Emily admits that there are times when she puts a lot of pressure on herself to succeed. And when she doesn't, she can get really bummed out at times. Those are probably some of her lowest moments, but she tries to talk herself out of them. She tries to not be so hard on herself.

What kind of **worker** are you?
Five ways to tell

1. Your teacher assigns you a tough research project. You ...
   A. Find it a challenging assignment and rush to the library to get started.
   B. Use the paper your friend wrote last year.
   C. Forget about it for a couple of days, then beg your mother to take you to the library so you can make the due date.

2. Your parents expect you to do chores around the house in order to get an allowance. You ...
   A. Do your work, most of the time without being reminded to.
   B. Hope your parents don't remember to check whether you've done your chores and give you your allowance anyway.
   C. Usually get around to doing it, although sometimes you need a reminder or two.

3. Your coach expects everyone to show up for soccer practices. You ...
   A. Try to manage your homework and baby-sitting so that you can make every practice.
   B. Go when you feel like it.
   C. Try to make most practices, but will miss a practice on occasion.

4. Your best friend asked you to go shopping and help her pick a cool outfit to wear for her birthday party. You ...
   A. Look forward to spending the time and helping her look her best - even if it means spending all day at the mall!
   B. Forget your promise - until she calls you to see if you're ready.
   C. Tell her you can only spend an hour.

5. Your younger sister is really struggling with her book report. You ...

A. Volunteer to help her.

B. Ignore her whining and hope she'll stop bothering you.

C. Decide, after hearing her complain for days, that you'll pitch in - if only to get some peace and quiet.

If you chose mostly A answers, then you are a very hard worker who is not afraid of responsiblity. No matter what job you do in life, you're a winner!

If you chose mostly B answers, it seems like slacking is a big part of your vocabulary. You need to dig in and do more for yourself!

If you chose mostly C answers, then most of the time you are pretty reliable and dependable. But there's always room for improvement.

Setting such high standards for herself does not always make Emily popular. "If I get an A and a friend gets a D, you can sense the tension - even if they don't say anything. Sometimes it's hard. My friends might not be that good at a subject and I am or my friend isn't as good at flute. Nothing is really said but I can feel it. I talk to my sister about it. I think she's been a really big role model, just being there. I just feel like I can tell her things," says Emily.

It helps to have role models. Role models are the people we look to and admire and hope to be like. Sometimes our parents are role models. Sometimes our teachers, coaches, neighbors, or brothers and sisters can be role models. If we're lucky, we'll have lots of role models in our lives showing us the way.

Emily says her sister is a role model. She's three years older than Emily and has been through three years more of living. Like Emily, her sister enjoys music - at 14, she's already been playing violin for **ten years!** She's a good student, has lots of friends, and is directed about her life. For these reasons, Emily is happy that she can trust her sister and tell her the most secret parts of her life. "I tell my sister everything I don't tell my parents," says Emily.

Her sister can give her advice and guidance, or just listen to her complaints, concerns, and cares. Because they're closer in age and share so many interests, they understand each other a great deal and accept each other. Her sister knows what it's like to be a sixth grade student these days because it wasn't so long ago she was one herself. When you try so hard and strive for so much, you also have to prepared for disappointments that will most surely come. Emily knows that we learn as much from our failures as we do from our successes. Maybe even more.

"Sometimes I write a huge paper, a good-quality paper. I don't even get it graded, but I feel good about what I've done anyway," says Emily.

She also sees barriers to girls' striving and success in very unlikely places. She says her gym teacher - a woman - won't let girls play football, because it's too masculine a sport. She also won't let the gym class play boys against girls - even though the girls want to compete against the boys. "I think some people don't ever give us a chance," says Emily.

That's the same complaint girls and women have had for a long time. Many women who have had successful careers say they feel they have to work twice as hard as their male colleagues to prove themselves because in some places attitudes still exist that suggest that women are not quite equal to men. But that's poppycock! Women and girls continue to prove that idea is all wrong, totally bogus, and unbelievably ridiculous!

I will be very happy. I'll be a zoo teacher who travels to schools with animals. MAYA, 11

When I think about my future I see myself as a nurse. I see myself married with a child, and I think I will be very happy. I don't know why I think of myself as a nurse as I can't stand seeing blood and gore. It makes my stomach churn when I see operations being done on TV. Well, you never know, maybe I will be a nurse! DONNA, 12

Well, I've always wanted to be a singer. Once I sang for Michael Barrymore. I sang in front of about 3,000 people. "I sang Always and Forever" by Eternal. JAYNINA, 12

I always think about my future. I see myself with my best friend in a mansion filled with pets, driving two cars, a silver Eclipse and a red convertible. We'll be working at a vet's, a marine place, and being a singer. ANNA, 11

Although Emily knows some kids her age that already definitely know exactly what they're going to do when they grow up, she's not really one of them. She has some ideas, but mostly she has the experience that's helped her figure out the kinds of things she enjoys doing. She knows she wants to go to college and she wants a good education. And between poetry, photography, art, and the flute, she can't decide. Maybe she'll do all of it, or maybe she won't. The important thing is, her parents, sister, and teachers have given her a strong foundation from which to build her future.

"My sister and I always used to imagine ourselves living in a big house together and our kids were best friends. **It's really nice because we're so close**." But what does the future really hold for Emily? Who knows? Even Emily - with all the wisdom of an 11-year-old - doesn't know for sure.

Check off which answers apply to you:

The greatest job in the world would be one in which I would ...

___ Make tons of money.
___ Enjoy the people I work with.
___ Love the work I do.
___ Work long hours.
___ Have a lot of say over my day.
___ Have a lot of responsibility.
___ Be considered a VIP (very important person).
___ Be helping people.
___ Work very SHORT hours.
___ Be the boss.
___ Work all by myself.

___ Learn something new every day.
___ Work with my hands.
___ Work with my mind.
___ Challenge myself.
___ Travel.
___ Become famous.
___ Be as creative as I could be.
___ Discover something new and exciting.
___ Feel that the work I was doing was making a difference.

9

GIRL TO GIRL

The Real Deal On Growing Up

I feel happy the most when I know I did something to be proud of, or something I know I did right. Especially if I go somewhere to represent a program or something. I feel the saddest when I feel like no one loves me or cares. People yell at me all the time. If I try to please someone, they always find something wrong with what I do. I let it out by crying. I'm really sensitive. I have to learn to deal with some of the problems I have and not always cry. LAKEISHA, 12

I think I feel most happy when I have accomplished something I've been working on for a very long time. Although I can't really think of a time when this has happened ... I just know it has. JESSIE, 12

LAKEISHA Age: 12

Lives with: her mother, a clerical worker, and her brother, nine.

Hobbies: dancing, basketball, soccer, volleyball.

Best achievement: winning a speech contest at her school about Maya Angelou, the black female poet.

Favorite subject: everything except social studies.

How she describes herself: "I feel great about my body. My hips are curved and I have a small waist. I'm tall but skinny. I also have blackish-brown wavy hair. My eyes are pointy from side to side. My skin color is brown. I have short clear nails and have nice muscle legs."

Enjoys: passing notes to her friends in school when she's bored.

Pet peeve: when boys in her school disrupt the entire class with their silly laughing.

Lakeisha is a typical 12-year-old. She is energetic, optimistic, and outgoing. She is very close with her mother but often has fights with her

I feel real happy when I spend time with my friends. I love it when my family spend time with me and we do things together. Actually I'm always happy because I'm a girl! I'm strong, smart, and bold! Most of the time I'm not sad because I don't let things get to me! I hate when people say girls or women can't do certain things. But I believe that women can do anything! I'm not planning on being the first anything. But if I could I would. SUKI, 11

I feel happy when I know I tried my hardest. In school, skating, horseback riding, and at home. SHANNON, 11

younger brother. She enjoys school very much, and has at least one teacher she feels especially close to. She adores music and dancing, hanging out with her friends, and watching funny movies. She is fun to be around.

She's going into the seventh grade and has already learned much in school. But Lakeisha also realizes there is still so much else to learn in order to grow up. In school and out. She is learning so much about herself, about her friends, about her family, about what she sees for her own future. Probably most important of all, she is growing in her understanding of her relationships. You know - how to **really** be a friend. How to stand up for yourself with a pesky brother. When to challenge a teacher and when not to.

Throughout this book, we have heard the many voices of real girls living real lives in real places. Girls who, like Lakeisha, are doing their best to grow up strong and independent and smart. Already these girls have accomplished much. These girls are changing every day. And growing up.

Being a girl IS different from being a boy. Our parents treat us different. So do our teachers. Our coaches and neighbors. Is that a problem?

No Way

Boys and girls are both trying to grow up. The challenges that each gender faces, though, might be a little different. Yet at the end of the road of their childhood years, both girls and boys are going to reach the destination of adulthood. The routes boys and girls take might be different. The things they see or think about along that journey might be different, but in the end, they will be at a similar place - even if they always look at life from their unique male or female viewpoint. The differences between boys and girls should not divide them, but should be something to celebrate and enjoy.

The Real Deal on Growing Up

Our job as girls is to figure out how to make the most of ourselves. How to be the happiest we can possibly be. How to achieve all that we want or can. In every area of our lives! It's not always easy, it's sometimes quite confusing, but here's the real deal: other girls are facing the same choices, meeting the same demands, sharing the same concerns. And when the going gets tough, the tough get talking. That's what girls do. They connect to each other and to themselves through talking.

That's why girls ....

... spend **huge** amounts of time on the telephone. They're connecting.

... Write their friends notes in school. They're connecting.

... Love staying up all night talking at a sleepover. They're connecting.

We have seen over and over again in this book, if there is one chief concern girls have, it's about their relationships. Am I part of the popular girls' group? Will I ever be friends with a boy? Is my best friend going to stay mad at me forever? How can I get my parents to trust me more? Why does my math teacher hate me? Who will I sit with at lunch?

Relationships are at once a mystery and the most natural thing in the world. Weird, huh?

Gal Pals

Lakeisha knows a lot about the mysteries of friendships already. For example, back in second grade Lakeisha first came to understand one of the things that separate a true best friend from one who isn't.

"A real friend doesn't make fun of you and call you names. The biggest challenge are secrets. You have to know who to trust. If you tell a friend something and you come the next day and the whole school knows, that's bad," Lakeisha explains.

One day she was at lunch, looking forward to sitting down with her friends and eating her sandwich, when she slipped in a puddle of spilled milk and landed on her butt. It was **awful!** She felt like the biggest klutz. She was sure the whole lunch room was watching her - which they were. But that wasn't the worst thing. The most horrible part of all was when her best friend at the time burst out laughing. Not just tee-hee laughter, but big loud guffaws. Like **ha ha ha ha**. The embarrassment didn't just stop with her best friend's laughter, she also blurted out so that everyone could hear, "How is your butt feeling now?"

"I was sitting in the milk. My best friend was like 'Are you okay?' But she was really cracking up. It's okay to laugh, but you can't be like cracking up," says Lakeisha.

The experience really made her look at the friendship and then take a step back from it. It hurt. It was a lesson in friendship Lakeisha has not forgotten. She now has a best friend she can truly count on.

"I can tell her anything I want and she won't make fun of me at all. She's younger than me but she's really mature for her age," says Lakeisha of the friendship she treasures so much. "I'm real goofy and she won't call me stupid or stuff."

I have one really best friend and then my other friends are all sort of equal, like I play with them heaps one day, then someone else the next. One of my friends said bronze friends are OK, silver are good, but the ones that she liked the most were gold friends. I think she meant best friends but I knew what she meant. ALICE, 10

I have a best friend. I like her because she has high self-esteem. A lot of my other friends always put each other down. Also she is trustworthy. She knows my deepest secret. Most of my other friends are fair-weather friends. We've all had our difficulties. My other friend one time broke a trust. I was hurt. I couldn't trust her. I had to tell her our friendship could never be the same. She accepted that and our friendship is in the process of rebuilding. ELAINE, 11

The times I feel happy are when I am with my friends and when they're giving me put-ups, not put-downs. That makes me feel happy. I feel saddest when my friends tease me or they won't tell me a secret and when they talk behind my back. The makes me feel sad because I feel like I have no friends. I have a best friend. She is my best friend because she is nice to me and never teases me. I have a few other good friends but no other one that comes as close to her. My other friends I can say hi to but I can't always trust them. KIM, 12

Boys Will Be Boys

Lakeisha knows a lot of boys. She sees them at school where, very often, they are showing off - pushing, shoving, and sometimes talking trash with each other. She's getting to understand that this is often how boys relate to each other - although sometimes she considers that sort of behavior just plain silly. She tries to be friends with them, although not always with success.

"Boys do not have much understanding of girls. Boys are much rougher and most don't think about what they say, but I hang around with boys. I don't hang around them much, though. A real boy friend is not a person to be scared of," says Lakeisha.

She hasn't had any boyfriends yet. She's waiting until it seems right for her. In the meantime, there is a lot to understand about them, and have them understand about her.

I don't think much about boys. I like my brother ... I like my two cousins who are 13 and nine. I don't really have much to do with boys. I mainly play with girls. At my old school I played with boys and girls. Boys are different from girls in lots of different ways. CAITLIN, 10

I don't really know a lot of boys. Probably if I was in a mixed school I would know a lot more boys. But with boyfriends I have had, well, some that lasted about a week and some lasted more than that. KELLY, 12

I have boys that are friends, boys that are best friends, and boyfriends. ALI, 13

My relationship with boys is very good because I have a brother who is the same age as me and I was really good mates with his friends. CHARLENE, 11

I have a little crush on a boy that doesn't go to my school but my church. The boys in my class, I have a great relationship with them. I talk with them and laugh with them. Some boys are really great friends. MAGGIE, 11

I like to be friends with boys but I don't like going out because it is dumb. And everybody makes a big deal about it. BRYANNA, 11

School Rules

School has been a laboratory of learning for Lakeisha - in many ways. Just like girls everywhere, Lakeisha has got to practice the skills she'll need someday as a grown-up. For example, she's already had a job at school. Lakeisha is on the school patrol, which means she has to be there a few minutes earlier before school starts and has to stay ten minutes later in the afternoon. Her job? To monitor the other students, make sure they are behaving themselves. "No running, no swearing, no doing rude things," she explains.

Lakeisha has proven herself to the teachers and principal. She is now a captain on the school patrol, which makes her feel really good about herself. She likes feeling that she is someone who is dependable. She wants others to count on her. And she sees how the school tries to encourage the students to be responsible and kind.

DEPENDABLE

"My school is fun because we can buy real things with fake money. We earn the money just by doing good deeds. Like if you answer questions, or are on the student council, or on the school patrol. We have a "Big Deal Book" so that if you do a nice thing, you get put in it. It might be being nice, saying thanks for something, picking up someone's pencil. Sometimes the teachers put their whole class in. You can buy pencils, hula-hoops, fake jewelry, notebooks, folders, crayons, or toys with the fake money," says Lakeisha.

Lakeisha loves school. She enjoys her classes and doesn't mind doing her homework. It helps her get the As and Bs she's proud of. "My teacher is really nice. She prepares us for the future and what's out there in the real world. She'll teach us about kindness. She's real sensitive. Sometimes she cries," Lakeisha recalls.

Her teacher was among those in the audience who came to a special program which focused on both black history and women's history. Lakeisha was asked to read a speech she wrote about Maya Angelou, a famous black poet who wrote a special poem for President Clinton's inauguration. Everyone in the audience; teachers, students, and parents, was all dressed up. Lakeisha's second-grade teacher came to hear her speech too. It made Lakeisha feel her future was wide open. She might accomplish anything she wanted. Just as Maya Angelou has.

My Body, My Self

It does hurt Lakeisha, though, when some of the other students in her school put her down for her achievements. One boy in particular has accused her of "acting white." She is African-American, proud of her skin color and her accomplishments. It is hurtful to be criticized for trying her best, but she tries to stay strong in her belief in herself. She speaks up for herself. It helps her feel more confident.

I like some of my teachers. My worst class is health. I'm pretty good at school.
MAEVE, 10

School is okay and the teachers are good but this one teacher thinks her kids can't do anything wrong. We have a small school with only 63 kids but it's good because you know everyone. We have 21 kids in our class.
BROOKE, 11

"I be like 'So?' I don't care. They expect me to act black, like swearing and wearing baggy pants. They call me 'teacher's pet,' says Lakeisha.

Lakeisha is learning how to stand up for herself and how to take charge of her life. She is learning to feel confident in her own ideas about things and express her opinion. She doesn't take no for an answer and she tries not to let those who oppose her bother her. For example, she and a group of girls at her school noticed how one girl **always** got to go to the library and help out. They thought it was unfair that one girl got special treatment when they all wanted to help. They decided to join forces and go to the principal to discuss the matter with him. They protested that it was unfair that one girl got to be secretary to the librarian when there were so many others willing to do the work.

"First we wrote him a note. I was shy, but I wrote mine like a job application. Now, we go to the library every day after we eat lunch," says Lakeisha. Their persistence paid off. They have the work experience to prove it.

Winning With Sports

With Lakeisha's height and athletic build, she's a natural basketball player. "Everybody says I'm tall for 12," says Lakeisha. She plays basketball with other girls at the girls club she goes to after school. It's a great outlet and makes her feel good.

Besides being fun, sports and other physical activity can boost self-esteem, making girls feel strong physically - and emotionally. Girls of color, like Lakeisha, who play sports are also more likely to score well on achievement tests, stay in school, and graduate from college. And Lakeisha is lucky - if girls haven't begun playing sports by the age of 10 as she has, only one out of 10 women are playing sports at the age of 25.

In addition to sports, Lakeisha likes to use her body to express herself by dancing, too. Sports is not the only way girls feel mastery over their own

My best friend is tall and hefty. She has a problem with acne and her mom won't let her wear makeup. I bought her some makeup for her 13th birthday and she's not even allowed to wear it. She looks gorgeous in makeup. I gave her a makeover when she came over once and she had to look twice before realizing that was her in the mirror. Isn't makeup what she needs to raise her self-esteem? She blushes really easily and is very sensitive to what people think and say. This isn't bad, though, because you can't get her to tell you the truth all the time.
HEATHER, 12

Well, I used to be worried about my skinny legs but when I look at some kids at school I'm glad I'm not large and I don't worry about it anymore. I'm happy with my facial features. I'm not exactly glamorous but I am kind of pretty in my own special way and everyone is special in their own way.
STEPHANIE, 12

bodies. For Lakeisha, dancing makes her feel connected with her own body and with music. "I want to be one of those dancers in the music videos," she says.

Physical activity is so, so important. Even if you're not active, you have to get out there and do something. I believe that's really, really important.
HEATHER, 12

Sometime I don't like sport and I don't like doing it that much. I don't like being competitive. I used to be pretty good at high jump but now I don't like it because I hit my back and hurt myself and now I am a bit scared of it.
CAITLIN, 10

Family: Got to Have 'em

Lakeisha has had a great life up to now, although it has not always been perfect. There are things that have happened to Lakeisha that made some bumpy places on the road of life. For example, her father doesn't live with Lakeisha and her mother, but lives in another city, which makes her sad sometimes. "We're not really close. But my dad's fun. He spoils me rotten," says Lakeisha.

Perhaps because her father is not around, Lakeisha and her mother have a closer relationship. "We have a really close relationship because she's a girl too. She teaches me right and wrong. She teaches me about pregnancy - about how when you get pregnant you can't go anywhere," says Lakeisha.

Lakeisha watches her mother. She knows how hard she works because she has seen her bring home extra work. She sits at the computer for hours filling out forms. She knows her mother wants her to succeed, to work hard and do well in life. Her mother has been a good example of being responsible and dependable.

Girls learn much from their first teachers - their family. It is the place of their first relationships. Lakeisha, for example, is trying to find a fair way to deal with her younger brother.

"We get along all right, well, not really that much because he likes to aggravate me. I think he must be bored. My mother says he must be bored. I yell at him. Or sometimes I just go in my room. That's why I'm glad I have my own room, my own space," says Lakeisha.

Trying to get along and not fight is a **huge** deal in families - especially with brothers or sisters, younger or older. Dealing with family conflict can help girls deal with conflict they come across elsewhere in their lives.

I love my family lots! They are nice! I am the youngest. GILLIAN, 8

There are four people in my family. It's me, my brother, my dad, and my mom. I'm the oldest child but I wish I had an older sister to talk to and clear the path for me. Sometimes my brother and I fight. Sometimes my mom and I fight. STEPHANIE, 12

What's important?

Rate these suggestions from most important to least important (1~10).

_____	Feeling good about myself
_____	My family
_____	Doing sports
_____	Being with friends
_____	Having fun!!!
_____	Standing up for myself!
_____	Boys!!!
_____	My future
_____	How I look
_____	Being ME!

My brother and I usually get along, unless I want to watch TV and he wants to listen to the radio. He really is my half-brother, but we like each other just the same. Sometimes he is grumpy when he doesn't get enough sleep. But he can drive me places, so my mom doesn't make me late.
MAEVE, 10

I like my family for the most part. I'm the oldest kid. My younger brother can be very annoying. I sometimes fight with my brother but we make up afterwards. Me and my brother get together good when it's just us and we're in a good mood.
EILEEN, 12

Future: There's No Crystal Ball

Right now, Lakeisha's most immediate concern in her future is seventh grade. She's going to a new school with new rules and new teachers. "I'm scared to go to junior high. I don't really know what's there," she confesses.

It's only the next of many, many challenges that await her. There will be many more choices, more successes, and probably some failures for Lakeisha. She is not sure what she will do later on in life. But whatever it is, she will do her best, try hard, and hopefully succeed. She's had many teachers in her life, beginning with her mother. And she expects she will have many more influences that will help her on the way to her future.

"In the future I see myself being a dancer in music videos, a singer, and an actress. I'll be married and have twins. I will be very happy and rich. I'll be happy going around the world to countries giving food to the less fortunate. I will be very proud of myself. My name will be known all over the world and have a monument or memorial. People will respect me and I would respect them, I would not be a filthy rich, greedy person. I will die knowing that I did something special for others. I'll die knowing that people are doing better because of me. I'll also die knowing that I made a difference. One person does make a difference. Don't make life miserable for others. Make life better for them," says Lakeisha.

I'll be happy. I don't know yet what I'll be doing in the future. I like a lot of stuff. JENNIFER, 12

Yes, I hope I will be happy. I have not made up my mind yet about what I'm going to do in the future but I love mathematics. ALICE, 10

I would see me as a primary-school teacher in the future. I have no doubts I'll be happy. I think I'll get married. SARAH, 11

Do you know yourself?

What better person to get to know than yourself? Discover yourself! Rate these 0~10 on how strongly you agree or disagree with these statements.

___I believe a good friend is someone I can trust.

___There will always be problems in relationships but talking always helps.

___I want a boy to be a friend before being a boyfriend.

___Parents need to set limits but it doesn't mean I always have to agree with them!

___Teachers are human beings even though they may act like aliens sometimes!!!!

___Being physically active or playing sports is important.

___To get where you want to go in life, you need to know where you are going.

___Strong relationships make me strong.

___I need to be my own best friend and I would never do anything to hurt myself.

___You should love being you!

Word Bank Can You Find?

school, teachers, classes, boys, friends, trust, relationships, family, parents, siblings, future, sports, physical activity, self image, fun, confidence, self-esteem, IQ, cool

```
P  H  T  R  U  S  T  M  N  I  S  M  D  F  A  M  S  R
H  I  M  D  F  W  L  I  S  A  T  B  O  Y  S  C  S  E
Y  I  S  N  O  S  O  B  I  T  C  R  I  J  T  S  I  L
S  V  H  O  Z  I  N  T  A  L  N  L  X  S  M  S  L  A
I  L  T  Z  E  I  F  I  M  A  G  E  A  M  L  I  M  T
C  V  N  M  T  H  H  A  D  W  I  Y  R  B  S  X  H  I
A  N  M  I  S  Z  S  D  I  F  Y  O  N  A  H  B  I  O
L  P  C  S  M  T  W  S  F  M  G  B  C  S  I  P  C  N
A  H  L  M  E  T  W  S  C  H  B  C  L  B  O  O  G  S
C  P  A  W  L  Z  T  S  I  Z  O  O  G  H  O  N  H  H
T  Q  S  R  F  I  T  I  Z  A  N  L  H  N  C  F  F  I
I  H  E  T  O  M  N  A  S  P  Y  G  X  I  T  I  Y  P
V  Z  L  S  N  M  S  P  O  R  T  Y  N  T  I  O  P  S
I  Q  O  T  B  T  B  M  C  T  C  X  I  S  N  E  V  I
T  A  R  Z  M  H  S  B  C  P  S  H  S  H  F  N  U  F
Y  L  I  O  U  Y  P  Q  R  G  R  L  H  C  O  C  M  U
W  X  S  N  O  P  Q  I  F  C  E  E  O  P  C  I  N  N
M  I  T  I  S  M  E  O  A  H  O  A  S  O  I  A  P  P
X  U  N  G  E  N  Q  T  M  R  L  F  H  R  A  L  K  L
E  S  I  U  G  T  N  I  I  E  F  T  E  U  E  E  V  A
A  P  Q  N  P  E  V  L  A  B  E  O  A  T  R  F  R  O
M  Q  P  S  T  U  V  W  Y  M  O  E  R  N  U  T  O  D
S  D  N  E  I  R  F  A  X  L  I  M  T  T  F  L  E  B
C  O  N  F  I  D  E  N  C  E  I  N  G  C  O  O  L  T
```

By sharing their experience,
girls just like you helped to make

Perhaps you have something to share!
Any ideas, comments, questions?

Please write to me in the UK in care of
Element Children's Books,
The Old School House, Bell Street, Shaftebury, Dorset, SP78BP

or in the US at
Element Children's Books,
160 North Washington Street, 4th Floor, Boston, MA 02114

or email me at
annedriscoll@compuserve.com.

G I

R L

G I